She hugged him, strong and soft at the same time, and tried to will some heat from her body into his. "Can you get up?"

"Got to—" He struggled. Got one cold, unfeeling leg under him and made it push. Helen steadied him and he got the other one where he wanted it. She pulled and steadied him some more till he was something like standing up.

"—got to kill that bastard Healey," he finished.

"Don't talk crazy," Helen said, "you're going to the hospital."

"Can't afford no hospital," he said. "Got to kill him."

"We'll go to the clinic on Fourth." She was motherly again. "We want to get you well. For Christmas. For the kids."

"Ain't going to Christmas." His voice was flat and cold now, almost as cold as his hands. "Just don't plan on going that far. And I ain't going to no clinic. Gonna get me a gun and kill him…"

EASY
Death

by **Daniel Boyd**

A HARD CASE CRIME NOVEL

A HARD CASE CRIME BOOK
(HCC-117)
First Hard Case Crime edition: November 2014

Published by

Titan Books
A division of Titan Publishing Group Ltd
144 Southwark Street
London SE1 0UP

in collaboration with Winterfall LLC

Print Edition ISBN 978-0-85768-579-7
E-book ISBN 978-0-85768-739-5

Design direction by Max Phillips
www.maxphillips.net

Typeset by Swordsmith Productions

The name "Hard Case Crime" and the Hard Case Crime logo are trademarks of Winterfall LLC. Hard Case Crime books are selected and edited by Charles Ardai.

Printed in the United States of America

Visit us on the web at www.HardCaseCrime.com

For Kathy

EASY DEATH

Before we get started...

This could be true for all I know.

A few years back I was cleaning out some old newspapers from the back room of a dead business—one of those mom-and-pop places that stays there for years, more from force of habit than for any profit involved. The newspapers were all from some small town I never heard of, and they dated back to when every little burg had its own newspaper, a radio station, two movie houses and a big marble Carnegie Library.

All of these papers were from right after Christmas of 1951, and they featured articles about the big blizzard of that year, the one that dumped a ton of snow all across the Northeast U.S., some places more than three feet in a single day. The paper said it hadn't kept Santa from coming, and the local businesses were doing all right, but Bud Sweeney's Used Cars was closed till New Year's in observance of the holidays.

There was also an article about putting up a monument to honor a park ranger who was killed in the line of duty—the editor seemed to think it was a great notion.

And down at the bottom of the page was a short piece that said the police had issued warrants for two local men in the armored car robbery of almost a week ago. There were pictures of them that looked like mug shots, one of them African American (but that's not what the paper called him, not back in 1951) and the other white, and the headline said SALT-AND-PEPPER TEAM SOUGHT IN ROBBERY.

Further down in that stack of papers was another paper, from a few months later, with the same picture and a headline, PAIR FOUND DEAD.

Just thought I'd mention it.

Chapter 1
The Night Before the Robbery

December 19, 1951
11:12 PM
Walter and Eddie

"The way I see it," Eddie looked out the passenger window into the night and took a last drag on his cigarette, exhaling smoke not much whiter than his too-pale face, "a job like this one tomorrow, you either go in and kill everybody first thing, or else you gotta sell them the idea of getting robbed."

"Yeah?" The man driving the ice truck shifted his big black hands easily on the steering wheel.

"Yup, and this what we're doing now is softening up what they call the sales resistance."

Behind the wheel, Walter peered out into the uncertain dark beyond his headlights, not really listening. "You figure?"

"Yeah, same as Mort and Slimmy on the tree tomorrow. Just doing our best to make for an easy sale."

Walter wanted to say something in polite agreement, but all he could think of was, "You know, I kind of wish I brought my gun."

Eddie crushed out a cigarette in the ashtray and looked at him with the edgy patience the State gives free to its long-term guests in recognition of their achievements. "You don't got one?"

"Brother Sweetie said he ain't for anybody to get killed this close to Christmas. Said it's bad for the job coming down, somebody get shot."

"Brother Sweetie, he thinks things a long ways out." Eddie looked out at the dim-lit streets as they passed. "Someone gets shot tonight, then tomorrow it's all over the news and everybody gets to looking over his shoulder and watching things close, and maybe they look twice at something more than it's good for us."

"Yeah, I guess." Walter sounded unconvinced. "I figured he just thought it was bad luck to kill somebody this close to Christmas."

"Could be it is," Eddie reflected, "but it's for sure bad luck to get yourself took dead this close to Christmas too, and you got a right to be worried about traveling light." He reached into his jacket and got the comfortable feel you can only get from having a Colt .38 Police Special tucked inside. "Does somebody see you out here this late, they see you driving this truck, maybe they figure you to be carrying money; they could stick a gun in your ribs, and that wouldn't do us no good either."

"That's facts."

"So I figure Brother Sweetie, he's a selfish sunuvabitch sending you out with no heat on a night like this."

"And that's facts too." The black man turned the truck carefully into an alley, looking to each side and checking his mirrors for any sign of something moving.

Nothing.

"You know he's got two cars?" he asked. "What's a man want with two cars when you can't drive only one at a time?"

"I better know it," Eddie said, "he puts me to greasing one or the other does he see me slow down at the garage any. And one of them a brand-new Hudson Hornet. Put him back more than a grand-and-a-half, he said." He looked out his own window as he spoke, scanning the streets on that side.

Nothing.

"Well you done good with this here truck," Walter said. "Can't nobody hear us coming nohow."

"Maybe too good." Eddie felt in his shirt pocket for a cigarette, remembered he didn't have time for it and fingered the top of the pack wistfully. "It don't really sound like a '36 Harvester oughta sound. Maybe just too quiet. Somebody sees an old piece like this moving so quiet, maybe gets to thinking about it too much."

"Could be you're just worrying yourself at it." The driver wrinkled his heavy brow thoughtfully. "Me, I like to drive quiet like this. You getting out here?"

"Yeah, but listen, Walter." Eddie rolled down the window, wincing as cold winter air flooded in, and he shifted in his seat. "You just ain't safe in this neighborhood at night." He slipped the Colt .38 from under his war-surplus Army jacket and passed it over to the driver. "You better keep this."

"You won't need it?" Walter slowed the truck as they approached a high chain-link fence next to a building with a picture of a Greek warrior holding up a sword and shield and under that a sign that read

AJAX ARMORED CAR
- Safe - Secure - Dependable -

"Not like you do." Eddie flexed his fingers inside dark gloves. "Just don't lose it or nothing."

"Well thanks, Eddie." Walter tucked the revolver under one leg, pinning it to the seat, and slowed the truck a little more, feeling the long gearshift lever slide easily as he worked the clutch. "See you later?"

"Does everything go right," Eddie said, and he reached out the window with both hands and drew his lanky frame onto the roof of the cab, then crawled up onto the square metal roof at the back.

The truck was down to a slow walk now, and crouching on top, Eddie looked down at the fence. Eight feet tall, with a strand of barbed wire running across the top, and a sign:

DANGER: HIGH VOLTAGE

And right beyond that, just inside the Ajax parking lot, the six squat, heavy-steel armored trucks parked in a neat row close to the fence.

He breathed in deeply, holding the air in his lungs, feeling the chilly small-town quiet like a cloak around him. Looked at the tight-coiled strand of barbed wire running the top of the fence and wondered if it really was electrified. It didn't look like it could carry anything more deadly than pigeon droppings, but... His hands shook a little and he looked down at them, wondering if the faint tremor was nerves or the seeping cold. He willed his hands to quit shaking, let his breath out slowly.

He looked at the fence again.

Then he rose and casually stepped over it, from the roof of the truck to the roof of the armored car on the other side. Slipped quickly down to the asphalt parking lot and crouched in the shadows to see if the noise of his entry had caught anyone's attention.

In a minute or so he decided it hadn't. He pulled a flashlight from the pocket of his olive-drab jacket and switched it on. The lens had been covered with windings of electrical tape until just a narrow sliver of light stabbed out in front of him, and he used this to check the numbers on the armored cars. Found the one he wanted, took a screwdriver from his pocket and set to work.

Five minutes later, he climbed to the top of the truck closest to the fence and jumped over, rolling with the eight-foot fall when he landed. Two minutes after that, he was walking casually past a radio repair shop at the edge of downtown, heading toward the gas station where Walter should be with the ice truck about now. *A cigarette would be nice,* he thought, *only this is maybe too close. Wait just a little....*

He passed the radio repair shop, hearing-without-hearing the music from inside that kept playing all night:

> *...To save us all from Satan's power*
> *When we were gone astray,*
> *O-oh ti-i-dings of co-omfort and joy*
> *Comfort-and-joy,*
> *Ohooo ti-dings...*

He caught the tune and hummed softly as he moved through the shadows. Two blocks farther he put a cigarette between his lips and got a Zippo lighter from his pocket.

A single snowflake touched his nose as he lit the cigarette.

Chapter 2
One Hour and Forty Minutes
After the Robbery

December 20, 1951
10:40 AM
Officer Drapp

That damned snow kept hitting the windshield like it had a special grudge against anyone dumb enough to drive in weather like this—maybe something against dumb folks as a general rule and me for certain—but I guess I was doing all right, considering the mess I was in. I took one hand off the wheel long enough to blow on it, pretending I could feel the warmth from my breath through the heavy leather glove and the knit-wool glove liner underneath.

And just kept driving.

I was piloting a pre-war Ford pick-up, and to judge by the dirt and manure caked on the sides, this was the first time it ever got off the farm since they shipped it down from Detroit. When I tried to push it over 30, the engine squealed like a pig in a sausage grinder, and the heater was just a tired old joke, but it was better for driving in this godawfulness than any police car I was ever in; the tread on those wide tires was sharp and deep, and six bales of wet straw in the back nailed it tight to the road. Even this road.

Yeah, this road.

It was the road they call the Willisburg Cut-off: all backwoods two-lane packed-down gravel, and there looked to be a foot of snow on it, and more coming down and coming down like God's judgment on this miserable sinner. Up ahead, I could see maybe twenty yards. Beyond that, everything just milk-white and blurry.

I looked down past the badge on my chest to the old radio bolted on the dash that kept fading in and out. I had it on looking to hear something about the robbery, but all I got so far was

I'm dreaming,
Of a wh-i-i-ite Christmas,
Just like the ones I uuuused to knoooow.
Where treeee tops glisten
And chil-dren listen....

No news reports on this station yet, and I didn't like to take my hand off the wheel again or my mind off the road to turn the dial.

And a good thing, too. I came up on a curve. Not a serious curve, but bad enough in this weather. I pushed in the clutch, hoping to coast slow enough so I wouldn't have to touch the brake and end up in a ditch on one side or the other.

It worked.

I down-shifted to second at the apex and let the clutch back out, pulling me around the bend and back in control. The road straightened out, I put her back in third while Bing was still crooning about every Christmas card he writes, and I looked ahead.

The tracks were getting easier to read.

Not that there was much to look at. Me and the getaway car were about the only things on this stretch of farm road between Willisburg and Boothe National Park, and the print of chains on those tires was hard to miss, the way they bit the snow like that.

Or maybe those tracks bit so deep from the extra traction of carrying a half-million dollars in the trunk. That wouldn't hurt any either.

I shifted on the seat, trying to get the big flap-holster on my right hip to sit easy on the worn bench seat. No use. Police uniforms are made for wear, not for comfort—same as this truck, I guess, so I might as well get used to it. There'd be more uniforms coming along behind me just any time now, so I'd do best to keep my mind on the road.

And the snow.

And those tracks.

I liked how they were getting sharper and clearer; that meant I was getting closer. Maybe not what you'd call catching up yet, but not falling behind any either. What with the lead he had, and all the fuss I ran into getting hold of this truck, I guess I was doing all right. Barring any accidents—his or mine—I was set to catch up with him in an hour or so.

And if I didn't, that wouldn't matter much because I knew where he was headed.

I tried to make myself relax some, not waste precious energy grabbing the wheel so tight, settle back and listen to Bing, who never got excited about anything in his life. Through the static he wrapped things up:

...and may allll yourrrr
Christmas-essss
Beeee white.

Chapter 3
Ninety Minutes Before the Robbery

December 20, 1951
7:30 AM
Logan and Chuck

The Pierce brothers, Logan and Chuck, walked out the door beneath the sign with the picture of a Greek warrior and the words

AJAX ARMORED CAR
- Safe - Secure - Dependable -

Logan blinked twice at the snow dusting the parking lot, shivered a little in the cold wind and nestled the company shotgun next to the folded newspaper under his arm. He pulled a toothpick from between his wide, white teeth with his free hand, pitched it into the snow and climbed into the back of the armored car, starched uniform straining across his wide shoulders and broad back. He kicked a little snow off his boots as he entered.

Inside the green-painted steel interior, he clipped the shotgun into the holder by the door, switched on the overhead light and turned on the war-surplus two-way radio riveted to the wall. Then, always feeling kind of uneasy about sealing himself in, he pulled the heavy door closed and shot home the bolt.

The sound of Chuck locking him in from outside came in quick reply.

He cast a glance at the empty space that would shortly be

filled with bags of money bound for Willisburg and points north, then settled onto the wooden bench against the front wall, stretching his long legs across the steel-reinforced floor.

"Hey how 'bout some heat back here?" he hollered at the wall behind him.

"Comin' up, Log'." The truck swayed—not much—as Chuck climbed up front and slid behind the wheel. Logan felt the rumble under his butt as the engine started and the radio up front gave out with

All I want for Christmas is my two front teeth,
Two front teeth,
Two front teeth,
Gee if I could only have…

"You ready for Christmas, Chuck?" Logan tucked his hands into his armpits and huddled for warmth as he spoke through the grate in the steel wall separating them.

"It's gettin' here whether I'm ready or not, I guess."

Logan worked his fingers inside his fur-lined gloves. "Somebody's getting ready for it; sounds like we got a big haul to Willisburg. Must be doing good business."

"That's all they think about anymore, is business." Up front, Chuck picked up a clipboard and began the ritual of marking squares on a mimeographed checklist as he spoke. "You remember Thanksgiving?" he called towards the back. "How Trudy had to leave before dessert just to get into Belkin's and start decorating? Didn't get home till near midnight, and next morning she's up at seven-thirty so's they can open the doors at nine ayem and not one minute later or old man Belkin might have conniptions."

"Well she did a real good job on that window. Looked real pretty this year. We took the kids to see it twice."

"I'd like to tell Belkin someday there's more to Christmas

than making money, and he can put that in his window and show it off." Chuck hesitated over a square on his list. "Hey, you gonna check that radio?"

Logan turned to the battered, olive-drab radio with the weathered stencil "U.S.A." still visible, and watched the tubes glowing softly. Picked up the black microphone hooked to the side.

"Jerry, this is Logan. Come in, Jerry. Over."

"Jerry here." The transmission was from the building right next to them, but fainter than usual. "Read you a little weak, Logan. Over."

"You're kind of weak here too, Jerry. Maybe there's ice on the antenna. Over."

"Could be. This snow supposed to amount to anything? Over."

"Lemme ask the brains of the outfit. Hey Chuck," he called through the partition, "we supposed to get much of this?"

"Not supposed to get any at all." In the cab Chuck stowed the checklist, then put the truck in gear. "I heard on the radio this morning just ahead of the Bob's Bandwagon show, and they didn't say nothing about no snow at all. Gonna get cold, though. Let's roll."

"Chuck says the weatherman says we're not getting any snow," Logan relayed into the microphone. "Must be your imagination. Over."

"Looks like an inch or two of my imagination, then. And I don't like the look of that sky in the west. You kids be careful now. Over."

"We'll check back as we leave the bank. Over and out."

Logan switched off the radio and settled back for the ride. Up front, Chuck eased the armored truck out of the driveway and onto the main road through town.

In the back it was starting to warm up a little. Logan relaxed and stared thoughtfully at the radio.

"You think we'll ever get shut of that war?" he asked.

"What you mean, Korea?" Chuck snorted from the driver's seat up front and called over his shoulder, "That ain't no war."

"No I mean the real war, the one we was in."

"We're shut of it now, ain't we? Been more'n six years we been home."

"Yeah, we're home," Logan said. "But seems like we're still there sometimes. Everything we use, it's war surplus. We buy a house, we get it on the VA plan. Go to meetings at the VFW. Hell, anytime I start to do something, I think back to how we used to do it in the Navy. Look how I just talked to Jerry on the radio here, same way we did it in the Navy."

"And what's wrong with that? Didn't the Navy way always fix something or make it worse?"

"Yeah, but…just seems sometimes like…we're home, and it's getting to be a long time ago…" Logan tried to make his point and found he'd lost it.

"I guess I just can't figure what you're complaining on." Chuck touched the brake and felt the truck slide gently and slightly sideways before it slowed, and he concentrated on driving, scarcely listening to Logan in the back.

"…my boy Jimmy, he starts first grade next year," Logan was saying, "and yeah, folks are gonna teach him about the war in school, but he's not going to remember it. Not like we remember it."

"Well how could he? He wasn't born then, was he?"

"Well he can't. That's what I'm saying."

"And so?"

"By the time he's our age, that war and the Navy way of doing it, that's just going to be his old man's story. But it was our life. We're never gonna be done with it, it feels like. But he's going to pick up and go on and never remember all that stuff, not like we remember it. He's not going to come on some problem or something and think back on what they told him to do in the war to figure it out."

"I guess not." Chuck had given up trying to get the point. "So are you guys coming over for Christmas?"

In the back, Logan thought back on Trudy's cooking, and the recent Thanksgiving feast. Remembered the dry, blackened turkey, so tough it hurt his teeth to chew it, and the soupy, over-salted stuffing.

"We'd like to," he said, "but the kids want to go over to Maggie's brother. They've got television, and they're crazy about it."

"Yeah, Trudy wants to get us one, and I guess maybe we might after Christmas."

"I wouldn't have one in the house. I know folks that got one and that's all they do all night is sit in the front room and stare at the damn thing. Don't much talk to each other no more at all. Just stare at the box."

"Some people, that might be an improvement." Chuck maneuvered the heavy truck into the parking lot at the rear of the Bootheville Federal Bank and up near the marble steps, just slightly smaller and less imposing than the steps out front.

"What kind of a family life is that?" Logan asked from the back. "If all you do is look at a box and don't talk to each other?"

"Not much of one." Chuck stepped on the clutch, moved the gearshift to "N" and set the brake. "Let's get out now and make a living."

Behind the bank, Logan stood with the shotgun across his chest, blinking snow out of his eyes as Chuck and a junior teller hauled bulging bags three feet wide and four feet long out from the vault, then piled them in the truck.

"Twelve bags." Chuck signed the form, wiped snow from it

and tore out the copy under the carbon paper to give to the teller while Logan locked himself back in the truck with the bags of money.

"Someone's getting a merry Christmas," the teller said. He brushed snow from his hair and shivered.

"Yeah, I guess," Chuck said.

Logan turned on the two-way radio again and got it warmed up.

"Jerry, this is Logan and Chuck. Over."

The answer sounded like it might have been in English, but that was all Logan could tell.

"Hey, Chuck," he called up front, "I can't hardly understand Jerry at all."

"Reception's always bad here back of the bank." Chuck rolled down the window and called, "Hey, Fred!" to the departing back of the bank teller.

Already at the top of the slippery steps and almost inside the door, Fred hesitated; he didn't much care to stand outside any longer, not in this weather, and he briefly debated pretending he didn't hear. Then he remembered it was almost Christmas and some childhood memory kicked in and told him Santa might be watching.

He turned. "Yeah, Chuck?"

"Call the office, would you? Tell 'em we're en route to Willisburg?"

"Your radio not working?" He thought uncomfortably of all that money inside the departing truck.

"Reception's bad back here," Chuck said, "and I guess this weather's not helping any. Would you call in for us?"

A blast of cold air made up Fred's mind. "Sure." He waved. "And merry Christmas!"

"Yeah, you too."

Inside the truck, Logan switched off the radio and braced

himself as they moved out. "We can check back in Willisburg, I guess." He settled himself on the bench and propped a foot on a money bag.

Up front, Chuck swore and tap-danced the brake as a car in front of them slid sideways. "Don't nobody remember how to drive in snow anyhow?"

"It'll get easier once we get off the highway and onto the Willisburg Cut-off," Logan said. "Nobody much uses that road anyhow, and a day like this…"

Sometime later, as the truck crossed over the railroad tracks at the edge of town, headed for Willisburg and points north, the radio antenna that should have been screwed tight to the roof swayed, bounced, and finally dropped out of its bracket. Out this far, there was no one behind them to see it stab into the thick, wet snow and bury itself.

Inside the truck, Logan talked of television, society, and the death of civilized conversation as they drove on into the deepening whiteness. Up front, Chuck ignored him, listening to the radio—

Here comes Santa Claus, here comes Santa Claus
Right down Santa Claus Lane,
Vixen and Blitzen and all his reindeer
Pulling on the reins….

Chapter 4
Two Hours After the Robbery

December 20, 1951
11:00 AM
Officer Drapp

The tire tracks from the getaway car took me straight where I knew they would: right through the main gate at Boothe National Park.

The road here got sheltered from the wind by thick woods on each side, so I didn't worry as much about snow drifts—not like I'd been bucking all the way up through that open farm country—but there looked to have been maybe another inch of snow in the last half-hour, and it wasn't for easing up any.

Boothe National Park covers about sixteen square miles of what is mostly woods, and this part here was what they call a scenic drive: easy slopes winding through the trees, and in nicer times it would have made a pretty sight I bet, but for pushing a clunky truck through deep snow, that road was just something else for me to cuss at, working the clutch in and out, down-shifting, brake-tapping and now and again just gunning the engine and feeling the wheels spin as that old beast crawled up those gentle inclines like Moses working a miracle.

This was getting to be too much like work.

Then all at once the woods thinned away and I pushed out onto open park grounds. Big playground and picnic benches, all covered in maybe two foot or more of snow, public toilets, signs I couldn't read for the snow stuck on them...the tracks in front of me just plowed through all of it.

And they went right past the visitor center.

For a minute there, I almost kept going myself. Then I got a glimpse of something parked beside the building. Hard to be sure in all that snow, but it looked like a Jeep.

That meant there was like to be someone inside, someone who'd maybe seen the car I was following and could tell about it. Also, it meant I might get a little help with this operation; that Jeep looked like a good bet for getting around in all this white slop. I put that up against whatever time I might lose going in there instead of following those tracks, and then I steered right, coaxing the truck through unbroken snow up to the building, close as I could get to the door.

As I got out, I undid a couple buttons on my coat and un-snapped the flap on my holster so I could get a hand in there quick did I need to. No sense taking chances with a job like this. I switched off the engine, cutting off Perry Como right in the middle of a long, smooth note. No question about it, the man could carry a tune.

Chapter 5
Thirty-Five Minutes Before the Robbery

December 20, 1951
8:25 AM
Mort, Slimmy and Sweeney

About a quarter-mile up the Willisburg Cut-off, just north of the main highway, Jack Mortimer took a deep breath of cold air and pulled again—and again—on his end of the long cross-cut saw, trying to make every ounce of his reedy body count for something. He felt the wind creep under his old felt hat and chill the thinning red hair underneath. Wet snow seeped through his cheap shoes. His hands stung and his back throbbed from the effort. He snorted, tried to swallow the snot that kept threatening to drip out his nose, and wished the snow wouldn't blow in his face. Wished Slimmy, on the other end of the saw, would use that pot-bellied flab of his better, and pull harder and get this damn tree cut down faster. Wished he'd never have to do a job like this again....

A few yards away, resting his bulk by the open door of his brand-new Hudson Hornet, feeling the warm air from the blowing heater turned up full blast, Bud Sweeney—sometimes called Brother Sweetie, but only very quietly and behind his back—looked from where the men were working by the side road, out through the woods to the main highway just beyond, then back to the half-cut tree, and finally at Mort, cold-sweating as he pulled the saw-handle.

"We all wish we weren't here, Mort. Faster you get the job done, sooner none of us will have to be." Sweeney's heavy beard and sharp brown eyes gave him a look somewhere between a college dean and a professional wrestler on television. Now he shifted the butt of a mostly dead cigar across his mouth as he spoke, scarcely aware of its presence.

Mort jumped a little as he pulled on the saw and wondered how Brother Sweetie always seemed to know what he was thinking. But instead of griping at him outright, he called over to Slimmy, "You just gonna ride your end all day?"

"Doin' as best I can," Slimmy whined, hands sore from unaccustomed effort.

Sweeney looked at the tree again, then back out at the road. Reluctantly, he left the side of the car, striding in thick rubber boots over to the tree. As the saw cut back and forth he studied the growing gash left in its wake.

"Leave off a minute."

He didn't have to say it twice. Slimmy let go his end and rubbed his hands for warmth while Mort pulled the blade back to him and out of the tree with a practiced, professional swing. Sweeney looked at the gash again, now more than three-quarters through the base of the trunk. He stuck out a leather-gloved hand and leaned his heavy body on the softwood above the cut.

The tree groaned and swayed. Sweeney leaned harder and produced a heavy, cracking sound. He pulled back.

"Good enough," he said. "Let's get in the car and rest up some."

Mort and Slimmy followed him eagerly across the road to the warm car and started to get in.

"Wipe your damn feet." Sweeney said it casually, over his shoulder, but both men stopped in their tracks and vigorously kicked the snow, sawdust and splinters off their shoes before they got carefully into the back seat.

"Now if that damn truck ain't late…" Sweeney passed a half-pint bottle of a reasonably priced whiskey back to the two men.

"Real thoughtful, boss." Mort took the bottle and carefully drank off just half before he passed it over to Slimmy. "Thanks a lot."

Sweeney didn't answer and Slimmy was too busy killing the bottle to add to the conversation.

"Lotta work," Mort ventured.

Sweeney said nothing. On his side of the back seat, Slimmy worked his tongue around the mouth of the bottle to get the last few drops.

Mort tried again. "I'm just saying it's a lot of work, that's all."

Sweeney turned in the front seat, moving his big shoulders around with surprising speed. "You said something?"

"It's work." Mort wished he had another swallow of the whiskey, but Slimmy hadn't left even a smell. "A lot of work. And cold out."

"Can't do nothing about the weather," Sweeney said patiently, "and if it wasn't work I wouldn't pay you for it."

"Like Mort here said," Slimmy chimed in, feeling the whiskey, "it's a awful lot of work for the money."

"You're right." Sweeney still sounded patient, but not by much. "I oughta just give the whole yard-and-a-quarter to Mort here since he did most of it, hadn't I?"

Slimmy made a sound that might have been a shrill belch or a low-pitched squeal.

"What do you think?" Sweeney turned his hard brown eyes on Mort. Then he took the cigar from his mouth before he spoke, a sure sign this was a special occasion. "You think we ought to just put little Slimmy here out right now and just you take his share?"

Mort could tell it was a trick question, but that didn't help him find the answer. He tried to look back at Sweeney, tried to meet the level, hard-eyed stare. But he didn't try it long.

"Guess not," he said finally.

"So you're happy with your share? Fifty bucks enough for your end of the saw?"

"Yeah." It was almost a whisper.

"And how about you?" This to Slimmy. "You happy with seventy-five at your end?"

"Yessir."

"Couldn't hear it," Sweeney said. "I'm asking are you both happy with what you're getting out of this association?"

"I am," Mort said eagerly. "Fifty bucks is just fine with me."

"Me too!" Slimmy added, "My–my share, it's just great!"

"That's real good." Sweeney was matter-of-fact about it. "Because I wouldn't want you boys to walk away from this job unhappy about anything." He paused. "I just couldn't have it." Paused again so they couldn't mistake his meaning. "You understand it?"

"Yessir." Both at once, like they'd practiced it.

"Real good." Sweeney stuck the cigar back in his mouth to signal the conversation was ended and all three men sat silent in the car, listening to the radio.

Ho-ho-ho,
Who wouldn't go?
Ho-ho-ho,
Who wouldn't go-o-o,
Up on the house-top click-click-click....

Five minutes later, the big grey-metal truck from Bootheville rumbled past.

"About time." Sweeney levered his door open and was out of the car before the two men in back had even moved. "You two just rest your delicate butts there," he said, "don't want you unhappy about doing any more work out here."

He walked across the road behind the car and leaned on the tree. It groaned and cracked. He leaned again.

That was all it took.

The tree went crashing down across the road, blocking it completely, the upper branches just missing the back bumper of Sweeney's car.

Sweeney walked back to the car and pulled open the door on Slimmy's side.

"Get to it," was all he said.

Slimmy jumped from the car and managed a quick "Right, boss!" like a soldier snapping to attention. Sweeney eyed him closely.

"That good liquor wasn't too sweet on you, was it?"

"Nossir!"

"You remember the spot, other side of the park?"

"Yessir!"

Sweeney felt a growing doubt and pondered the wisdom of just doing it himself, but all he said was, "Don't call me *sir*, I work for a living."

"Yess-uh…. Right, boss!"

"Now, I'm asking do you remember the spot on the far side of Boothe National?"

"Sure do!" Slimmy shook the whiskey-buzz from his head and concentrated. "You drove us out there twice, dincha? Just last week."

"And you can get there? The snow won't bother you none?"

"Boss, I was born in Minnesota, and up there we wouldn't even call this snow, we'd—" Slimmy found to his alarm that the booze had made him talkative, and he sensed quickly that Sweeney wasn't happy with it. "Don't have no problem getting through something like this at all!"

"So get there."

"Yeah-uh…" Slimmy felt the cold and hugged his arms quickly. "Uh, boss, how long you want me to wait there, I mean, uh, in case…."

"In case of what?"

"I mean if they don't make it. How long you want me waitin' out there?"

The snow blew a short white blast in his face to underline the question. Sweeney looked out at the growing misery-weather.

"They got to stop the truck and get the load; that's gonna take some time maybe," he said, "then they get to the park and get clear across with it, and in this weather, that's going to be a while longer I'm guessing…." He paused, like a man adding sums in his head. "But however long it takes 'em, they'll be counting on having you sitting there at the other side to collect. And I'll be counting on that, too. You understand it?"

Slimmy nodded. It made him a little dizzy, trying to concentrate on Sweeney's words.

"So if you leave before they get there—if they get there and you're not parked right there waiting for them, however long it takes—you better hope all this has melted off by then, and there's a lot of grass growing between you and me." He measured off a level stare and pushed it at Slimmy. "Understand it?"

"Yessir!"

"Then git!"

As he marched through the deepening snow to the wood-paneled '41 Ford parked out by the highway, Slimmy told himself again and again how much he hated working for Brother Sweetie. *Well there's ways of making it easier.* He felt the full pint-flask of gin bouncing deep in his coat pocket and smiled to himself. *That sunuvabitch don't know everything he thinks he knows!*

❋

And as Sweeney drove his sleek and shiny Hudson Hornet through the deepening snow on the highway back to Bootheville, Mort sat patiently in the back seat, hearing,

> *It caaame upooon a mid-night clear....*
> *That gloooriousss so-ong of olllld,*
> *From annngels be-ending near to Earth,*
> *To touch,*
> *Their harps....*

and feeling glad he didn't get stuck with Slimmy's end of this job, and planning what he was going to do with his fifty bucks.

Chapter 6
Ten Minutes Before the Robbery

December 20, 1951
8:50 AM
Logan and Chuck

Seated on the hard bench, riding backwards, long legs out, feet propped on a money bag for stability, Logan Pierce studied the newspaper.

"Chuck, you ever read this comic strip *Pogo* here in the funnies?"

"Is that the one with the talking alligator?" In the cab, Chuck slowed for a curve, moved the wheel gently side to side to keep control in the thickening snow, and picked up speed again as the road cut deep into the woods where the drifts would be less trouble.

"Yeah. Well, I guess they all talk," Logan said. "It's full of animals talking to each other."

"No, I don't never read those little-kid comics."

"Well I can't put any sense to it. Sometimes they don't even talk English. And the lines—you know the lines around the little boxes?—the lines aren't even drawn straight."

"I never read it." Chuck eased off the gas pedal for another curve. "I just read the grown-up comics. *Dick Tracy* and *Steve Canyon*; that's a good one. And *Little Orphan Annie*."

"I like that one myself."

"Yeah, you know, she's just a little kid, but sometimes she says something that'll make you think."

"She sure does."

"And speaking of which, you thought any more about what I said last week?"

"Some," Logan admitted.

"So whatcha think?"

"I dunno." Logan laid the newspaper down on the seat beside him and fished a toothpick from his pocket with big, blunt fingers. Chewed on it thoughtfully as he spoke. "Don't see much point in it, I guess."

"No point!" Chuck's voice rose, and Logan said a quick prayer that he might not put the truck in a ditch. "You want to be shuffling other folks' money around all your life when you could be helping out your town and make something of yourself maybe?"

"You mean get myself dead maybe." Logan kept his voice soft, hoping not to excite Chuck. It worked. *Or maybe Chuck's concentrating on driving in this mess.* Logan hoped so. "Being a cop, that's dangerous work," he finished.

"But the pay's better." Yes, the voice was steadier now. "And I'm thinking it's no more dangerous work than this job here."

"You ask me, it's lots more dangerous than this job here," Logan said evenly. "All we do here, you think on it, what this job is all about is we put money in this here truck and if somebody tries to take it, we shoot 'em. That's it. Nice and simple, you ask me.

"But if I was to become a cop," he went on, "well then I gotta bust up a bar fight or walk down a dark alley if I hear something, stop some guy maybe beating up his wife and when I sock the guy the wife socks me or I don't know what all, but it's dangerous work."

"But the pay's better."

"What's a cop make, anyway?"

"Drapp told me he takes home near seventy dollars a week."

"Yeah, but that's Tom Drapp, and that's in Willisburg. Drapp, he come back from the war with a bronze star so he knows his way around trouble, and he's been working there how long? Five years maybe?"

"Like that."

"And us, we been here four years and bringing home more than sixty every week. Now where's a guy like me gonna find a job to pay like that?"

Chuck's voice rose again. "On a police force, you big simple."

"Look, all I'm saying, it's dangerous work, that's all. A man like Drapp maybe he makes it look easy, but it just ain't. You read in the *Citizen* last September about the murder of Gonzago?"

"Everybody read that," Chuck snorted, "you couldn't read about nothing else for a whole week. And it just goes to show what I said about getting on the police force."

"It don't go to show nothing of the kind," Logan said calmly. "You read in the paper about Chief Hannon making the arrest and everything, but look a little closer: Anybody could tell it was Tom Drapp did all the work on that case. Took some smarts, too, but Drapp, he's sharp. And if he'd get along with Chief Hannon a little better, he'd be in plain clothes now instead of still driving a black-and-white."

"So what are you saying?"

"I'm saying cop work takes brains and guts and hard work, and this job here all it takes is a certain amount of guts. And no brains at all, no hard choices to make. See?"

"And all I'm saying is all we do all day is sit here like a lump of fubar in a plate of fubar stew and— Heads up!"

"Whatcha got?" Logan felt the hairs rise on the back of his neck as Chuck slammed the clutch and tapped the brakes.

"Looks like a police car up ahead. Flashing light's going."

"Maybe they just couldn't wait to hire us up."

"Could be an accident most likely. Hold on, there's a police-man out, he's flagging us down. Better call it in."

Logan was already at the old radio, flipping the switch and waiting for the tubes to warm up. Eventually, the tiny speaker emitted a soft, featureless blur of noise. He keyed the micro-phone.

"Jerry, this is Logan. Come in, Jerry. Over."

The only reply was static slush, soft, thick and featureless—like the snow outside.

Up front, he heard Chuck roll down the window. "What's going on, Officer?"

"Man's pinned under the car." The officer's voice sounded tense and out of breath, but still authoritative. "Need help up here—fast!"

"Stay here, Logan," Chuck called into the back, "while I check this out."

Logan felt the truck rock a little as Chuck jumped out while he repeated into the microphone, "Jerry, this is Logan. Come in, Jerry. Over."

And all he got was the same soft nothing for an answer.

Logan looked at the microphone, then at the radio, lips tight, brow creased. He started to call again, but—

"Logan, get out here!" It was Chuck outside, shoving the key in the lock and twisting it fast. "We got to move this car or some guy's a goner!"

He hesitated, still perplexed by the silent radio.

"Logan—Come *on*!"

He grabbed the shotgun from the rack and swung the metal door cautiously open.

Outside, Chuck was struggling to keep his balance in shin-deep snow and pointing a frantic finger to the front. Ahead of him, a man in a police uniform glanced at the shotgun in Logan's hands, waved a commanding arm like a man used to directing traffic, turned and started wading through the snow toward the flashing bubble of red light on his car.

Logan leaned out the door a little further, still clutching the shotgun, and looked up the road. About thirty yards away, under the police car, between the front and rear wheels, a pair of legs lay in the snow, twisted at an odd and painful-looking angle.

It was enough for Logan. He clipped the shotgun back in the holder and jumped out, stretching his long legs through the snow to catch up with his brother.

Halfway between the truck and the police car, it occurred to him to wonder how a man might get trapped under a police car on a remote stretch of road like this. But he kept wading through the snow.

So he was almost even with Chuck when the man in police clothes spun around with a gun in his hand.

Chapter 7
Two Hours and Fifteen Minutes
After the Robbery

December 20, 1951
11:15 AM
Officer Drapp

It took maybe a half-minute for me to get out of the truck and into the ranger's cabin, and all that time the wind hit me like it was throwing bullets: big wet freezing-cold bullets to cut at my face and cover my dark-blue coat with a sheet of white. I got in, slammed the door behind me and tried to catch my breath.

Inside it was like you'd expect in a park. All logs and knotty pine walls, not big, but empty enough to look roomy. In one corner there was one of those big old-time radios, squeaking out

Star-r-r-r of ho-oly beauty bright,
Westward le-eading,
Still procee-eeding,
Guide us to….

On the wall behind me, they'd put up a couple of those wooden racks full of maps and bright-colored guides to the local attractions. In front of me, a plain pinewood desk gave the place a solid, official look. There was a ranger sitting at the desk with his back to me, talking on a phone about something, but I couldn't hear much of it with the wind howling right outside. I kicked my feet on the wall, shook a couple inches of wet snow off my hat and shoulders, and stomped another few pounds off the soles of my boots before I clumped over to the desk.

And while I did that, the ranger put the phone down, stood up and turned to watch me track the blizzard across his floor there.

"I'm Officer Drapp," I said, "Willisburg Police."

The ranger was big; taller than me and broader-shouldered, big and outdoorsy-looking, with a tan that hadn't faded even in December. In a brown shirt stretched tight across big shoulders, the brass buttons sparkling like he shined them for a hobby. Only it wasn't a he. She stood up behind the desk, showing a crease on her pea-green pants sharp enough to open a letter with, and from the wooden hat tree behind her taking one of those hats like Smokey the Bear wears.

"Is it still snowing out?" she asked in a voice soft as silk.

"Tell you the truth, I hadn't noticed." I shook another half-pound of it off my shoulders and tried to get a better look at her without being too obvious.

Now, in the movies, a guy sees a woman doing the kind of job at which there is usually just guys, he takes a step back and says something real brainy: "You're a girl!" he says, or like that. But I wasn't real sure. First thing I thought when I saw her was that does a man have a horse and it's a really fine horse, and he likes it enough, well if he wants to dress it up like a park ranger and put it behind a desk, that's his business. Next it started to come up on me that maybe this wasn't a horse after all, any more than it was a man, and finally, a few long split seconds later, I figured out what it was—

"My name's Callie," she said, "Ranger Calpurnia Nixon, but I hate that name so it's just Callie."

Her voice sounded like that one from the movies, I can't think of her name, but she's skinny and not bad-looking and she always plays classy parts and she says all her *R*'s like they was *H*'s. I'd seen her in this one movie just a while back where she's some preacher's kid or something, and she's in Africa or someplace and looking like you could keep ice cubes in her mouth, all white paint and primroses, and next thing you know she's jumping Humphrey Bogart.

Like I say, I can't think of her name right now, that actress I mean, but that's how this Callie talked, all soft and high-class, and you couldn't believe it come from that big ugly horse-face. Her nose was way too large to start with, and it had got broke at least once and wasn't set good. Around that nose, her face was hard-skinned and squared-off: big eyes, wide mouth, strong chin, and she had cheekbones like to poke your eye out. She wore her brown hair short, and cut like a man's.

"I'm afraid we just closed—but you don't look as though you came here to enjoy the park." The words came around her big teeth like it was someone talking behind her.

"Not today." I kicked the last of the snow off the tops of my boots. "There's some tire tracks running past here."

"There are indeed."

"Did you see what made them?"

"Why—are you following someone?"

"You see what made them?"

"Oh, I didn't answer your question, did I?" She sounded really sorry about it. "No, I heard a car go by, the only one today, but by the time I got to the window it was out of sight."

"How long ago now?"

"You are following someone, aren't you?"

I didn't ask again. Didn't trust myself to do it nice. Just looked at her patient-like till she picked up on it.

"I think—and I'm not saying I know—I think it would have been more than half an hour ago, but not quite an hour yet." She said it carefully, like she was really trying to get the time right. "When I hung up the phone I just now said to myself *I have to go out and look for them.* We just closed the park, but I told you that. Why are you following them?"

"Not them," I said. "Him."

"Just one man?"

"Just one man now. A couple of guys, they held up an armored car on the state road south of Willisburg. On the cut-off there. I got one, and I think those tracks out there are from the other."

"Don't you know for certain?"

"Pretty certain. Not a lot of tracks to follow out there today."

"Does that make it easier?"

"Not really. Can I trouble you for that Jeep outside?"

Chapter 8
The Robbery

December 20, 1951
9:00 AM
Logan and Chuck

"Stop there and hold real still, friends." The voice of the man in front of them, the one in the police uniform pointing his gun their way, was still calm and commanding, but somehow much different.

Logan stopped.

Chuck stopped.

Both their hands went for the guns at their sides.

And froze motionless as they heard the unmistakable sound behind them of a round being jacked into a shotgun.

"Like he said, friends," the voice at their backs a little bit deeper and a lot more scary, "hold real still."

They held real still.

The man in the police uniform with the gun in his hand walked a few steps closer, his long blue coat almost touching the snow, heavy boots moving carefully. Logan studied the gun, noting it looked like a .38 Police Special revolver with a four-inch barrel. Standard issue in just about every police department he knew of. The man himself looked lanky and a little pale, and Logan wondered for a second if he might slip and fall, then wondered what the one behind them with the shotgun would do if that happened. He hoped the man didn't slip and fall. Tried to swallow and found his throat suddenly dry.

And he needed to blow his nose. He sniffed noisily.

"Wipe it on your sleeve." The pale man seemed calm and understanding, almost like Logan and Chuck's stern father, if their stern father had packed a gun. "Just do it slow."

Slowly, Logan wiped his nose on his sleeve. From the corner of his eye he saw Chuck doing likewise.

"Pay attention now." As the man in police clothes spoke, Logan heard the edgy patience in his voice; like he'd heard before, in the Navy, from twenty-year veterans so used to giving orders that the thought of disobedience never entered your mind. "I say pay attention here friends, 'cause your life hangs on it."

Logan paid attention.

"In an hour or so," the man said, "when you don't show up in Willisburg, do they come looking for you two, they'll find you locked up in the back of that tin-can truck there. Now they can find you alive or they can find you dead, and that's all up to you and how much trouble you give us."

Logan looked into the man's eyes. They looked hard, professional, and surprisingly honest. "You do just like we say and you come out of this alive," he was saying. "Either one of you make us any trouble and they'll find your brains spread out here, if they look real hard for them once the snow melts. And I'll give you something else: I never killed a man in my life and left any witnesses around to remember it."

Logan sniffed again and wiped his nose on his sleeve. Very slowly.

"Big fella," the man said, leveling his pistol at Logan, "take the sidearm out of his holster—" the gun waved a fraction of an inch toward Chuck "—and throw it over there in the snow. Use your left hand. Do it slow. Not fast."

Chuck sniffed, trying to keep his nose from running in the

cold, and wondered if the man would think he was crying as Logan reached slowly over and took the gun from Chuck's holster. He hoped the man wouldn't think he was crying.

Chuck lowered his right arm a fraction of an inch. "Slip it to me!" He hissed the words to Logan without moving his lips. "Then jump right. I'll jump left and go for the guy behind us."

Logan hesitated, calculating his chances of handing Chuck the gun, jumping right, pulling his own gun and shooting the man in front of him.

He tossed Chuck's sidearm in the deep snow.

"Now you there," the man in the police uniform said. He nodded at Chuck. "What's your name?"

"I forget just now." Chuck tried to return the man's level gaze and found it difficult; he thought maybe the gun had something to do with it.

"Well Mister I-forget-just-now, there's something on your face, and I don't much like the look of it." The man was almost smiling, but not quite, and it made Chuck feel frustrated, like when he was little and told all the grown-ups how he was going to be a policeman someday and arrest all the bad guys, but no one took him seriously, and *why am I remembering all that right now?* He sniffed in the cold and wiped his nose on his sleeve again.

"...so when you take your partner's gun," the man in the uniform was saying, "I want you should use your left hand, just the fingers, and move it real slow when you toss it away. You understand that, Mister I-forget-just-now?"

Chuck didn't say anything. And he didn't move. Behind him, the other robber said softly, "You want me to just go ahead and kill him?"

The man in the uniform didn't seem too concerned. He didn't act like they were in a hurry or anything like it. He just stood there in the blowing snow without seeming to notice the cold, and then he grinned outright.

"You know, I'm not for killing the both of you today," he said easily. "Not for it much at all." He raised his voice a notch, "But Pinky there behind you with the shotgun, he wouldn't mind killing you boys too much. Would you Pinky?"

"Don't mind it at all." The voice from behind them didn't sound amused or friendly. "You just give the word."

"Well I guess he don't mind it at all," the man in the uniform said. "But me, I just hate to kill even one man. You know, I killed a man one time and then I didn't get to sleep almost all night, it bothered me so much. I like to been up almost half the night before I got to sleep, and all over killing just one man."

His voice dropped and all the humor went out of it.

"So I'm going to say it once more. This ain't your party, bud. It's my party, and I'm playing the tune: take your partner's gun and throw it away. Slow."

Chuck wanted to say, "Go to hell," but he couldn't think of it. So he just stood there, defiantly still.

A second passed as the snow fell around the men standing knee-deep in the empty white road. Then the man in the uniform cocked his service revolver.

Logan felt his stomach lurch. He tried to make his voice work. "Hold on, mister," he managed, "just hold on, I'll do it myself." He crossed his left arm across his body and reached the holster on his right hip. "See, I'm doing it slow," he said, "you don't have to shoot anybody, I swear we won't make trouble."

The man in the uniform seemed to like that better, but he kept his eyes on Chuck as Logan awkwardly took the gun in his left hand, holding it by the barrel, and brought it back across, to throw it away.

It passed close to Chuck's raised right hand, the butt just

within easy reach. The man in the uniform seemed to read the future in Chuck's eyes, and it didn't bother him. He was ready for it.

Logan wasn't. A shock like an electric jolt went through him as Chuck snatched the gun out of his hand and swung it around toward the man in the uniform. Moving in slow motion, Logan turned his head to stare at his brother in disbelief.

He was just in time to see the right side of Chuck's head explode in a red burst.

Chapter 9
Two Hours and Twenty Minutes
After the Robbery

December 20, 1951
11:20 AM
Officer Drapp

Getting hold of that Jeep was more work than I figured on.

"You may not need it." The ranger got a thoughtful look on that big hard-featured face of hers. "Captain Scranton is on the tower and of course he might have seen whoever made those tracks, and he can tell us what they look like; and then you can call in the description from here, and they'll be waiting to pick them up as they come out the other side of the park. That should work just as nicely, shouldn't it?"

"No, I'm afraid not." Not for me, anyhow.

And anyway it sounded kind of funny from where I was standing. I didn't know much about how these park rangers work, but I couldn't see any boss of the outfit sitting up in a lookout tower and letting the wonder-horse run things down at headquarters here. And come to that—

"What's anybody doing in the lookout tower on a day like this?" I asked. "You can't see anything more than a half-mile off, can you?"

She looked awkward at that. And I mean it was like she'd sat on something sharp and couldn't move her butt off it.

"Oh, he's out there, I'm sure." She turned away from me, more to hide her face than anything else, it seemed like. Then she walked, kind of like the way a cowboy walks in the western movies, over to an old-style crank phone in a wooden box on the wall, pulled the earpiece up to her ear and turned the handle like that should change the subject. I heard the phone jangle through the earpiece.

"Captain?" she pitched her voice into the mouthpiece and cradled the ear-part tight against her head—it was either to hear better or to shut me off from asking any more questions. "Captain Scranton?"

And then she just stood there, listening at the phone while nobody answered.

"Captain Scranton?" She turned the crank that was supposed to sound a bell on the other end and tried a different tune: "Emergency here. Captain Scranton, this is Ranger Nixon and we have an emergency here, I'm afraid. Could I speak to you, Captain?"

I guess not.

She didn't even try the phone again, just hung it up and turned to me and said, "Well I suppose we must take the Jeep out after all."

"You're half right," I said. "I'll take the Jeep out and look for my man out there, and do I find your Captain, I'll have him phone in."

"Well that won't do." She said it like she was looking at a smudge on her coffee table. "No, I shall have to go with you."

"Can't have that," I said, trying to sound patient. "I'm after an armed robber and—"

"And that's all well and fine for you I'm sure, but Officer Drapp I just this minute lost my Captain and I've got to find him. Now if you're worried about me, I'll put on my sidearm, but—"

"But I don't take any civilian on a job like this, especially not—so don't even talk it over with me. This is a police matter and—"

"And you almost said *'especially not a woman,'* didn't you?"
She shot a look at me that stepped all over my face for what she
thought I was going to say—and all over every man who ever
said that to her. Or anything like it.

It was some look, that look.

"Well, I have responsibilities of my own," she went on when
she could do it without spitting at me, "and at this time that's to
find out what's become of Captain Scranton, and I really don't
care how many bank robbers you need to chase after."

"He's not a bank robber; they hit an armored car."

"Car or bank or gumball machine is neither here nor there
as far as this conversation goes." She squared her shoulders,
stuck out her lantern jaw and lowered heavy eyebrows at me
like she was swinging a club or something, "I must go after my
captain."

And I saw we were all done talking about it. My chances of
getting that Jeep without her in it was cut way down to nothing,
unless I knocked her down and tied her up, and was I to try
something like that the smart money would all be on her side.

"Better get that sidearm," I said.

Even that wasn't quick and it wasn't easy. She had to mess
through a drawer to turn up a key that went to a cabinet with a
lockbox inside that had the key to a gun locker. It was a pretty
impressive gun locker, too, steel-reinforced, with a high-powered
hunting rifle inside keeping company with a shortened-up shotgun and an army surplus Colt .45 automatic. All this time I tried
to look patient and listen to the music from that big old radio,

…the cattle are lowwwwing,
The poor baby wakes,
But little lord Jesus,
No crying he makes…

Well good for Him. I made myself say something nice. "Looks like you take good care of the weaponry here in the woods."

"We never lock the building itself." She released the clip from one of the .45s, checked it, shoved it back in and hunted up a holster and belt. And she did it like someone who's done it enough to make a fast, professional job of it. Made me wonder how well she could handle the business end.

"We have tourists and campers coming in here for all sorts of things," she went on while she worked that gun, "and sometimes even an animal wanders in, and of course we don't want the animals hurting themselves. So we keep the guns locked up as best we may."

She went through the Chinese-puzzle-box of locking everything back up again, then put on a giant fur-lined Eskimo coat. The coat made it so she couldn't have got that .45 off her hip in less than a quarter-hour, but it looked thick enough it likely could stop a bullet.

"There." She pulled a parka hood over her head that just about covered her face, and lumbered around a little. "I feel just like Nanook of the North."

She looked more like one of his sled dogs, and not the lead dog neither, but I just said, "Better let me drive; I'm not sure you could move your arms in that thing."

"Good idea," she said. "Do you want to call police headquarters for help before we start out? Or perhaps just let them know where you are?"

Not much I didn't. And I'd wasted about as much time here as I could.

"Wouldn't work," I said. "Let's go."

She gave me a funny look. "You're going after these armed robbers all alone?"

"Just one armed robber is what I think."

"And you're going after him by yourself," she pressed, "without calling for more men?"

"Wouldn't work." I said it again so she'd know I meant it.

"Well, I guess being a police officer, you're no doubt used to walking into danger."

"You reckon?" We started to the door.

"I just happened to think," she said all at once, "was anyone killed in this robbery affair?"

"Just about." I opened the door and let the wrath of God hit me in the face. "It was pretty close."

Chapter 10
The Robbery

December 20, 1951
9:13 AM
Logan and Chuck

"Ahhhh! You bastard!"

Chuck screamed and kept on screaming, and as the noise went on, it began to slowly dawn on Logan that neither of them was dead. He looked up from where he lay face-down in the deep snow as Chuck sank to his knees, hand clamped to his right ear and filling with blood. He was bellowing with pain and rage and fear.

"Whudja do to me, ya sunuvabitch?"

"I shot your right ear off," the man in uniform said. He took a careful step forward and retrieved Logan's fallen gun from the snow, then pitched it into an even deeper snow drift a few yards off. "And did you think it was a lucky shot," he continued, "just hold your head still and see me trim back the left ear to match it. But you best stop all that hollering first, 'cause it might spoil my aim."

"Well it hurts, damya!"

"Maybe you figured it should tickle?" The man turned slightly to Logan. "Mister, shut him up before I have to do it."

The way he said it—like a teacher telling you two and two makes four and no argument about it—kicked Logan into gear. He got up from the ground, wet snow still caked to his face, and reached out his arm to his brother.

"Chuck, for God's sake, c'mere," he said.

They were both on their knees, Chuck still holding his ear and sobbing, "Log', look at what he done!"

"It'll be all right," Logan said evenly.

"It won't!" Chuck whined. "We letting them *rob* us, dammit! We lose our damn jobs over this! Who gonna hire a man with just one ear? Who? Dammitdammitdammit they might as well just kill us now as—"

And Logan, still on his knees, knocked his brother out with one punch.

"Nice work." The man in the police uniform looked down at Chuck, motionless and silent in the snow. "Now find something to tie up his head so he don't bleed to death. And move slow when you do it."

Logan got handkerchiefs from his pocket and from Chuck's, unsnapped Chuck's clip-on uniform necktie and untied the fake knot, then began bandaging his brother's ear. It was slow work, and in the end he had to just hold the wadded cloth against Chuck's head to stop the blood.

Behind him he heard the second robber pulling bags out of the truck and sliding them through the snow to the big trunk of the police car, which he could see now was just an old taxicab painted black and white, with a flashing light stuck to the top and a pair of towel-stuffed pants and boots underneath to look like a run-over body. Six bags fit in the trunk and another five in the back seat. That left one bag still in the armored truck, but there was no room for it.

"Get inside," the policeman said, "and get your partner there with you."

Logan dragged his brother through the snow, in the grooves left by the money bags, and tried to lift him by the shoulders into the back of the truck, but he was too heavy. The man in uniform watched him struggle with the weight for a few seconds, then pointed his revolver at Logan.

"See this?"

Logan nodded.

"Well remember I got it."

He tucked the revolver into a pocket of his long blue coat, in easy reach, then grabbed Chuck's legs at the knees and helped get him into the truck.

The man in the police uniform stood by the door while, inside the cargo bay, Logan towed Chuck to the back wall, propped him half-up, crouched beside him and looked at the handkerchief-bandages. The bleeding seemed slower now. He felt the truck shift as the man in the police clothes climbed in and drew his gun.

"How's he doing?"

"He'll be okay, I guess," Logan said.

"Well, prop his head up."

Logan took off his coat, shivering a little, and used it as a pillow to elevate his brother's head.

"And make damn sure he don't die, 'cause then I got to come back and kill you over it." The man sat down on the bench at the front of the small money-cab. "Now take out your wallet and his too and slide them over to me."

"The hell you say—robbing the truck ain't enough, you gonna rob us, too?"

"I didn't say we should discuss it." The man in uniform said it like a lecture he had delivered many times. "I said get those wallets out and slide them over to me. And do it slow. Then turn your back to me."

Logan did. A minute later, the man in the police uniform said, "This guy, he's your brother?"

"That's right."

"He still lives on Gate Street there in Willisburg?"

"Yeah. How you know?"

"It's on his driver's license. And you still live on Plovis? In the new part there?"

"Yeah."

"Get you a place on the on the G.I. Bill, did you?"

"Yeah."

"Nice place is it?"

"I like it."

"Any kids?"

"What the hell is it to you?"

"Nothing at all." The man in the police uniform tossed the wallets back. They landed in front of Logan, next to the unconscious Chuck.

"But I'm going to give you this," the man in the police uniform said, "I know where you live now. And I know where your brother lives. So when they come and find you, you tell the cops what you saw made you stop was an ambulance. Got that? You stopped for an ambulance. It was white with a big red cross and it was an ambulance you stopped for. And a man got out, he was dressed in white like a doctor or something and he was short and you think he was blonde and that's as much as you saw of him. Hear me?"

"Yeah."

"Then you say it back like I said it to you."

"We was driving and Chuck he stops when he sees an ambulance ahead in the snow. And—"

"What's the ambulance look like?"

"It's white and there's a big red cross."

"Go ahead."

"And a guy got out dressed like a doctor and he waved us down."

"And what else did you see?"

"I don't know."

"What else did you see?"

"Nothing. The guy he was dressed like a doctor, kind of short and I think he was blonde, he pulls a gun on us and then he–he shoots…." Logan felt himself choking up. With surprise, he realized he was close to tears, holding his unconscious brother.

"That's enough. That's fine. You did real good," the man said behind him. "So when your brother wakes up you coach him real good to say it just like you said it. And that's the story you give come the time they find you. We got a police radio in the car there, and do I hear any descriptions get out that sound like us, well…" He paused.

Crouched with his back to him, Logan felt a shiver of fear.

"…we know where you live," the man finished.

Logan didn't trust himself to answer. He was too close to tears he couldn't understand.

The man in the police uniform kicked the last bag of money gently with his foot. "Just a damn shame, having to give that up," he said, "but I guess there's no sense being greedy."

Logan felt the truck shift as the man in the uniform got out, slammed the door and locked it from the outside.

Then there was just the darkness and Chuck breathing heavily as Logan held his brother's bloody head. And cried.

Chapter 11
Thirty Minutes After the Robbery

December 20, 1951
9:30 AM
Mort

About the time Slimmy reached his rendezvous point on the far side of Boothe National Park and found a spot to pull off where he could begin his drunken vigil, Mort was standing in front of the big oaken desk inside Bud Sweeney's Used Cars, feeling the warmth of the office-and-garage seep through his thin coat and dirty shoes. He held the long cross-cut saw awkwardly half-under one arm, while Sweeney rooted around in the cash register, pulled out a single five-dollar bill and laid it into his outstretched palm.

"A fin?" Mort blinked.

"The way I count, it makes fifty," Sweeney said, "and that's how you count it too."

"C'mon, Mr. Sweeney," Mort juggled the saw comically as he looked down at the battered bill and then up at the big man, "you said fifty! You said it just this morning and it was hard work...."

"And that's what you're getting," Sweeney said. "But not now and not from me. You go flashing a whole lot of bills around and folks'll think Christ hit town. Or Santy Claus come early to your place. Or maybe they'll think something else funny come up about this time."

"Guess you don't want that, huh?" Mort sniffed and wished he had a spare hand to wipe his nose with.

"I don't," Sweeney agreed. "And you don't, either. Understand it?"

"I guess."

"So you take this fin and you go find Boxer Healey. He ought to be back of Lola's today."

"Healey?" Mort managed to shove the bill in his coat pocket, pull out a dirty handkerchief and blow his nose, all without dropping the saw. "What do I want with Boxer Healey?"

"He got a card game going, don't he?"

"Healey's always got him a game going," Mort said. "Hell, he makes his living—"

"Well today ain't his lucky day." Sweeney said it like God passing judgment. "Because you're going to take that five and put it in his card game and you're gonna run it up to fifty."

"Yeah?"

"Yeah, and then Healey's gonna get mad and throw you out of the game. He just ain't gonna play with you anymore. Not today, anyway. And if you got any brains, you're gonna quit and walk out of there, and if anybody asks how a bum like you got his hands around all that money, you can say you got on a lucky streak back of Lola's. And likely there'll be witnesses."

"Damn." Mort almost gasped in awe. "Mr. Sweeney, you sure think things way ahead!"

"So now you know how to collect your fifty bucks, do you?"

"Sure do." Mort smiled. "Hell, I already spent it!"

"How's that happen?"

"I need ten bucks to square the rent, ten for the heat, I want to give Helen ten for groceries... We put some stuff on layaway, you know, stuff for the kids on Christmas, that's seven-fifty more. And I plan on getting me some new shoes. Work boots, I mean. A good five-dollar pair. And a couple pair of those heavy work gloves: the dollar kind. Then I'm gonna ask Magruder to get me back on the tree-trimming crew."

He looked outside as another white gust dumped more snow on a street that already had plenty of it. *Magruder's gonna need men*, he thought. *And need 'em fast. He'll put me back on, sure. I do this right, he'll hire me on steady. Then I'll be drawing a paycheck regular and we can feed the kids a little more and dress 'em up good so they don't have to feel ashamed around the other kids at school, and…*

He looked at Sweeney, but Sweeney had already lost interest.

…and I won't have to work for no miserable sunuvabitch anymore!

He started out the door.

"Mort." Sweeney used his I'm-being-real-patient voice, and it stopped Mort short in his tracks.

"Yessir?"

"Leave the damn saw here."

Chapter 12
Two Hours and Fifty Minutes
After the Robbery

December 20, 1951
11:50 AM
Officer Drapp

The Jeep outside the ranger station was a Willys Overland, the kind I spent two years taking apart and trying to put back together again for the U.S. Army, first in Italy, then France, then in Germany. Right after the war Henry Kaiser took a bunch of these and screwed metal boxes with windows to the top and tried to sell them like they were cars, but he didn't fool anybody much; an Army Jeep is about as close to a real car as a three-legged Missouri mule is to Seabiscuit. Anyhow, the sight of this one, as we shoveled two feet of snow off the flat steel top, was kind of reassuring. It didn't exactly bring back fond memories— I didn't have any from those days, none at all—but it was good to know I'd have wheels I could handle in a job like this.

"Have you run it any today?" I had to shout over wind that bit the words out of my mouth and flung them across the park like a mean dog, but Callie nodded she'd heard me just fine.

"I opened the main gate about five this morning, before all this snow started," she said, pitching her voice to reach me through the blowing white slop, "and I went out again about two hours ago to check the cabins."

It shouldn't take too much coaxing to start up then. I nodded and jerked the ice-frozen door open, pushed my way inside and behind the wheel as Callie shoveled out a track behind the rear wheels. I sat down, and sonuvagun if I didn't get that old familiar feeling I used to get back in the war. When your butt hits down on the cold plastic seat of a Jeep like that, you can feel the devil bite your ass and tear him off a big hunk.

Okay, so it wasn't warm in there, but it felt better just being out of the wind, and I took a few seconds to get my face thawed out while Callie stayed out there and dug up more snow. I looked around inside, and it was the stuff you'd expect in a park ranger's Jeep: first-aid kit, a coil of rope under the front seat, army blanket, that kind of stuff. I checked the gearshift to see was it in neutral, jerked the parking brake from force of habit, set the choke and flipped the switch.

There was a short, tired growl from under the hood. Then a cough. Then a sputter. Then another growl, longer this time. Two more coughs, and all at once the engine was running, with that deep-throated whine that belongs to a Jeep, and underneath that the sound of a radio going,

...on the feast of Steee-phen,
All the snow lay round about,
Deep and crisp and eeeven,
Brightly shone the moon that night...

I turned it way down while I let the Jeep get used to the idea of running for a minute. And while it was doing that, I got an idea myself about just driving away while Callie was putting the shovel back up against the ranger cabin. I didn't do it, though. For one thing, she was packing a sidearm, and for all I knew she might just be able to get it out and object to the notion of me leaving like that. For another, this damn snow was getting awful deep, and could be I'd get stuck someplace and need something big and brutal to push me out. Like her.

So I waited till she got in on her side, then let out the clutch and next thing we were barreling forward, to the end of the track she'd shoveled out for me.

Didn't work. Not at all. We hit the end of the track and just stopped, all four wheels spinning in the snow.

"My." She shot me a level stare, like I'd done something stupid, which I guess I had, kind of. But all she said was, "Aren't *we* in a hurry!"

"Yeah, I guess we are," I said.

She didn't answer, and that was a smart move on her part. I slammed in the clutch, put it in reverse and backed to the other end of our track, waited till we hung up there, then shifted gear back into forward and we shot off again. This time we made it beyond her dug-out track a ways before we stopped. I lurched the wheels backwards into the snow, then forward, then back, then seriously forward and got us moving. Jeep-moving, I mean: bounce twice for every bump you hit. "Do you know the way to the watchtower?" she asked.

"No, but I'm young and willing to learn. Do I start to turn wrong just grab the wheel and jerk it."

She laughed, and it made a dainty little sound, like she might have learned how to laugh like that in finishing school.

"You know my father did that to me once," she said, "while he was teaching me how to drive."

"Wha'd you do?"

"I simply let go of the wheel, crossed my arms and put my foot down on the accelerator." She said it like it was a cherished memory. "Poor father," she sighed, "I guess I put him through rather a lot."

So she was a gal that liked to talk. Which was good, because there was something I wanted to get at: like maybe the look on her face when she started to say about this Captain Scranton, and how she didn't answer when I tried to ask what the hell he was doing up in a watchtower on a day like this. But they didn't seem like the kind of questions I could just ask head-on; I figured to get there slow and sideways.

"So what are you doing for Christmas?" I asked.

She looked surprised. Maybe she didn't figure cops asked questions like that. "I have a cousin in California." That soft, cultured voice of hers still sounded funny coming from someone her size and shape, but I was getting used to it. "He's doing rather well for himself, and the family's meeting at his place for Christmas. I'll take the train the day after tomorrow. Or rather, that was my plan...."

"You worried about your Captain?"

She didn't answer right away. And I could see now she didn't give a hoot in hell about the man. Something else was eating at her about him, though. I told myself to take this slow.

"I got a cousin myself." I squeezed the gas pedal just a touch as we went into a rise, trying to get just that extra push without making the wheels slip. It worked. The road straightened out and we rolled along in the almost-covered-up track of the car I'd followed all this way. And I kept talking:

"My cousin Handy, he's got a diner in Presque Isle, and every Christmas he closes up and invites just the family in and that's where do we have Christmas, in the diner there. Makes it nice, kind of different with the whole family there and the Christmas decorations up and everything."

We came up on a curve, but I didn't have to let the clutch in; just eased up on the gas and felt the four-wheel pull us gently around it till I could straighten out. The wipers couldn't do much about all the snow hitting the windshield, but the heater was starting to help some and we couldn't see our breath in the air anymore. The insides of those GI Jeeps can get hotter than the hinges of Hell, which would be pretty much what we'd need on a day like this one.

"Your cousin in California," I went on, "he's got a nice place?"

"He's a senator." She said *senahhtahhh* like she was yawning or something, "And people like to give him nice things. His wife even got a new coat last year." She managed to put two syllables into *year*. "So I suppose it's rather nice for them, but I'm afraid the holidays…well, an awful lot of persons in business seem to drop by."

"He have kids?" I figured to keep at her till she really got to talking. "You bringing presents?"

"Two girls," she said. "And I asked myself, well what can I possibly get little children with rich parents? And then it struck me: I bought a dog, a black-and-white spaniel, and I know what a terrible chore a dog can be, but I've got Checkers trained and house-broken, and I think she'll be a wonderful companion for the girls, don't you?"

"I guess I know what you mean." I tried to steer her like I was steering the car: nothing real sudden, just gently now. "How about your Captain Scranton? He talking about any holiday plans?"

She turned up the radio. "Don't you just love the Christmas music they play this time of yee-ahhh?"

Hark the herald angels si-ing
Glory toooo the new-born king,
Peace on Earth,
And mercy mi-ild…

I some way kept myself from choking the steering wheel, un-clenched my teeth, took a deep breath and tried to get her talking again.

Chapter 13

Callie Nixon

Callie turned up the music and tried not to let her mind go back there. Tried to listen to the inane prattle of that pasty-faced city cop.

It didn't work.

She kept seeing it again, her first meeting with Captain Scranton, driving into Boothe National Park, into the glare of a clear sunrise, feeling the cool morning summer air on her face as she got out of her shiny black Studebaker station wagon and looked around. Her surprise at not finding her new boss in the ranger station.

Then hearing that awful noise.

Even now, riding in that cold jeep, just thinking of that sound still set her teeth on edge. The keening high-pitched drawn-out *"Ho-oo-nk! Hoo-ooo-onk!"* coming from behind the building. She found the back door and ran out to see the bloody feather-crushed Canada Goose trying to move with its legs and wings broken.

And the man smiling down at it.

Holding an axe.

He had a square, stocky football-player's body and sandy blonde hair cut in a flat-top slicked back with Vitalis. His olive-drab ranger uniform had drops of blood on the trouser cuffs that hadn't soaked in yet, shining bright red above his brown combat boots.

She took all that in, or tried to. Tried to understand that the man smiling as he watched the animal suffer was her new boss. Tried to realize what that meant.

But all she could say was,

"Lord, kill it!"

And she didn't know if she was swearing or praying.

"They taste better if they suffer first." He didn't look at her; he couldn't take his eyes off the flopping thing on the bloody ground. "When they struggle like that, it pumps the blood up," he went on, still watching it. And still smiling. "And the slower they die, the better they taste."

He ran his tongue across his lower lip, like he was already gorging on it.

Callie wasn't even aware of moving. Never knew how she pulled the axe from his hand and swung the blade down across the goose-neck in one smooth, fast motion. By the time her head cleared she was already standing at attention, holding the axe upright like a soldier on parade and saying like a formal announcement,

"Ranger Calpurnia Nixon reporting for duty, sir!"

And that was how it started.

Chapter 14
The Getaway

December 20, 1951
9:15 AM
Walter and Eddie

"…Like I said, a job like this, it's like you was selling something," the man in the police uniform said.

"You still reckon it like that?" Behind the wheel of the car that looked a little like a police car, the man in the red hunting coat turned his dark face to him, grinned quickly, then turned his attention back to the snow-covered road piercing the woods.

"Yeah, that's the way I see it: you either go in shooting and kill everybody first thing," Eddie said from the passenger side, "or else you got to sell these guys on the idea of getting robbed."

Eddie thought about lighting a cigarette. Instead, he opened the cylinder of the Colt Special, flipped out the spent shell, and put it carefully in the pocket of his long blue police overcoat. He loaded a new cartridge in the empty chamber, snapped the cylinder shut and slipped the gun back in the flap holster. "I was a kid, I sold stuff door to door for money. I learned quick you got to size a guy up fast and talk to him like he talks to you; get to him personal, you know."

"Okay."

"Then you figure out what does this guy want, and whatever you're selling, you tell him that's it: it's what he wants. And it's the same thing on a job like this."

"So you sell these guys on us robbing them?"

"You sell them on the idea of staying alive, is what you do."

Eddie shifted on the seat, trying to get the flap holster to hang comfortably off the right side.

"Well, I guess that one fella, he didn't much want what you was selling." Walter eased in the clutch on a curve, then let it out again and gained as much speed as he thought might be safe.

"I guess not." Eddie shifted his butt again, and then gave it up. "Seen it in his eyes, him thinking if he didn't try something and try it now, he wouldn't get another chance. But I'm glad I didn't kill him, kind of."

"Well you sure know how to work a gun, and that's facts." Walter smiled. "Shot his ear clean off! Seen it go fly through the air an'—where'd you learn to make a shot like that?"

"You think that was a good shot?"

"That's facts."

"I was aiming at his shoulder."

"His shoulder? You was? Well it was still awful slick; seen that ear of his go flying through the air like *that*—" Walter flapped one hand across the dashboard, then quickly back to the steering wheel. "You sure got the winning way about you!"

"Just glad I didn't have to kill nobody."

"And that's something else. Way you talked back there about killing. Scared 'em like to death. Just about scared me too, come to that. You really ever kill somebody?"

Eddie thought for a minute. "I dunno, Walter. I really don't know. Shot some Germans once, but I sure wasn't going up to them right then to see did they die from it. Anyway, I'm glad we didn't have to kill nobody. Brother Sweetie would've give us hell did we kill a man on this job."

"And that's facts," Walter said. He took a deep breath and made himself concentrate on the road. The tire chains rattled and pounded through snow as the woods thinned out and turned into farm country. Beyond the woods, across the open fields, the snow was turning into drifts. Deep drifts.

"Can you handle this?" Eddie fished a cigarette from his pocket.

"Not much choice in the thing. Got to handle it. We get stuck out here and lose all this money, Brother Sweetie'd kill you slow and me slower."

"Too true." Eddie pulled a Zippo lighter from his pocket, held it to the end of the cigarette and set fire to it. He drew the smoke deep into his lungs and let it out slowly through his mouth and nose, filling the inside of the car with a yellow-grey cloud. "Brother Sweetie's one unpleasant sunuvabitch to work for, but he sure can organize a job like this." He rolled down his window just a crack and saw the smoke cloud sucked quickly out.

"You think he really can open those bags?" Walter asked. "I hear tell you can't cut 'em with a knife."

"That stuff they're made of, you couldn't even shoot a bullet through it. He'll likely need a torch to cut off the locks, but he'll do it. That's why he's the brains of the outfit. Too bad he's a sunuvabitch."

"Yeah, that's awful tough on him." Walter looked quickly over at Eddie's cigarette, then back at the road again. "Hey gimme a drag off that, will you?"

Eddie took the cigarette out of his mouth, put it between Walter's lips and held it long enough for the other man to inhale. "Let me know do you want another." He put it back in his own mouth and took another deep pull, letting the nicotine calm his nerves.

"Thanks." Walter applied light pressure to the gas pedal as they crossed a snow drift, gently pushing the car onward. "And you're right, it's a damn shame about Brother Sweetie. I guess a man in his line, he's got to be tough, but he don't got to be no sunuvabitch. And he getting all this money. Just hope he don't find out we had to leave a bag behind. How much you figure we got?"

"I'm thinking maybe seventy-five grand."

"And you and me only taking home five, and we done all the work."

"You figure that?"

"Well, I didn't see Brother Sweetie out there holding no shotgun."

"He don't have to hold no shotgun." Eddie took another deep lungful of smoke and spoke thoughtfully as he exhaled. "You got any idea how much he worked just to set this up? Got the dope on that truck, lined up the car and fixed it up to look like this…. Hell, he even had me to put chains on the tires this morning when he saw it was snowing. I tell you Brother Sweetie's got brains, he has."

"Well don't *we*?" Walter slowed as they approached a bend, feeling the heavy car slide way too close to the drain-ditch on one side, then straighten out. He breathed a short sigh of relief. "You ain't saying we didn't use our brains none?"

"Walter, on a job like this, you and me, we're just the moving men. Just the hired help, that's us. Brother Sweetie wants someone smart enough to get the money and scared enough to give it to him, and we fit the bill just fine. That's you and me."

"You reckon? Worth no more'n dogs wages?"

"That's about it. All we are is moving men and that's all we ever will be. That's why I'm getting out of this line of work."

"You know," Walter wrinkled his forehead in thought, "that's most likely a smart thing, too." He steadied the car against a windy broadside, thankful for the weight of the money over the back tires. "Getting out. It's a smart thing and that's facts."

"Well nobody robs folks forever without they get caught doing it sooner or whenever. That stretch I did learned me that much. Do I go up again, well I'm fixed for life, and I don't fancy spending out my years playing rock hockey in a striped jersey. That's how come I figure just to take my pay and go my way." He studied the shortening cigarette. "You want another drag before I pitch this?"

"Thanks but no." Walter shook his head. "So what you gonna do?"

"Guy I know, he's got a gas station on a sweet little corner just outside Akron. Needs a partner, a mechanic partner, I mean, and I figure to buy in with him. Akron's a good town for fixing cars."

"You gonna make a living fixing cars?"

"Yup. You can make good living at it too, when you run your own place, I mean. That's how come I to know Brother Sweetie, working on those heaps he cuts up and sells out, but I don't figure to spend my life working for him. And Akron, it's one fine town for fixing cars."

"Yeah?"

"Sure is." Eddie took a last gasp on the cigarette, hot to his lips now, and reluctantly stubbed it out in the overflowing ashtray. He rolled up his window. "They make tires there, you know. And they got bad winters, which is good for a mechanic's trade."

"Well you can fix cars, Eddie, and no doubt about it. Never knew somebody to cure up a car like you."

"It's about the only thing I learned in the Army was fixing cars." Eddie reflexively felt in his pocket for another cigarette, but decided against it. Regretfully. "I just been looking for someplace I could work for myself. Not work for wages. This job comes off like it should, I'll do it, too."

"Makes sense and that's facts." Walter looked like he had

something on his mind, but before he could speak, Eddie asked him,

"So what are you doing for Christmas?"

"Going to visit my brother's wife. Down south a ways. My brother, he's dead, a little time back. She got a house full of kids will be glad to get some new clothes and maybe a toy or something."

"You going to play Santy Claus with the kids?"

"Ain't going to spend it all show-boatin'." The road curved and Walter eased his left foot gently down on the clutch. As he did, the shotgun on the floor at his feet slid forward. "Hey move that thing, will ya?"

Eddie bent forward. "Nothing wrong with playing Santa Claus." He picked up the shotgun by the barrel, and, keeping the muzzle carefully pointed away, jammed it between the bags in the back. "Just don't go blowing all your money, that's all."

"Well, Jesus said to help the poor and be nice to little kids, didn't he?"

"Yeah but I ain't heard him talking it up lately."

"How about you?" Walter let the clutch out again. "What's your Christmas?"

"I don't know. Family, I guess."

"You mean Brother Sweetie?"

"Hell no. That miserable low-down sunuvabitch ain't kin to nobody." Eddie spat on the floor. "I got family upstate, I can do Christmas together with them."

"Should be nice."

"It will be, do I get there," He looked out at swirling white all around them and wiped the window with a blue-sleeved forearm. "We don't freeze to death out here and get buried in snow, it ought to be nice."

Behind the wheel, Walter tried to concentrate on his driving and not worry too much over what else he had on his mind.

Chapter 15
Three Hours and Thirty Minutes
After the Robbery

December 20, 1951
12:30 PM
Mort and Healey

In the room back of Lola's, Mort ran a hand through his thin red hair, looked down at his cards, then separated two from the hand and set them on the table.

"Gimme two?" he said.

Across the table, Boxer Healey peeled two cards from the deck, his gnarled, big-knuckled hands amazingly deft at it, and flicked them across the table with bent-up fingers.

"Gimme one." The man on Mort's right laid a card on the table without much enthusiasm and picked up another with equal disinterest.

"I'll keep these." Howard from the barbershop held his cards close and kept checking again and again to make sure they hadn't changed. Healey looked at his face and decided there should be a rule against doing that, just to keep the game from getting too predictable.

He looked back at Mort. "What you gonna do?" His jet-black face creased open in a carefully staged smile below his broken nose, a smile made up especially to show off the single gold tooth shining out from a bed of ivory-white.

Why's he smiling? Mort looked nervously to his left at Howard from the barbershop, then at the heavyset grey-haired stranger on his right. Then down at the loose pile of five-dollar bills on the table. *Is this my pot? Does he really mean me to take it?*

"You need to think it over, Mort?" Healey's voice, which never showed anything he didn't want it to show, sounded a little impatient. "Because if you want to take a walk or something and turn it over in your mind, well, me and the boys here, we'll watch your money for you. Won't we guys?"

The others laughed dutifully.

Mort felt himself redden. "I call," he said.

The grey-haired man on his right showed his cards. "Three fives."

Howard from the barbershop laid his hand down. "I guess that beats a pair of tens."

Across the table, Healey folded his cards. "I got nothing." He stretched the long, powerful arms that got him his name, and leaned back, displaying the soft belly that had ended his career so spectacularly five years ago against Archie "Mongoose" Moore in the Arena.

Mort stared in disbelief and laid down his cards. "Four nines."

"Yeah?" the grey-haired stranger tried to sound surprised. "Thought I had that one."

Mort pulled the bills to him like he was doing it in a dream and rifled them with his fingers. *Fifty bucks… Damn, if Magruder hires me on, I'll be bringing this home every week. Think of that? Me bringing home fifty every week to…* He counted again. Eleven of them! *I'm even five bucks up! Why now I can buy —*

"You done us good that time," Howard said. "Four nines! I never knew you could take on Boxer that way, Mort!"

"He done us for sure," Boxer nodded, his pride hurt. "Can't believe I let old Mort do me out of a pot like that."

Mort tried to read the black man's eyes, knowing he wouldn't see anything Boxer didn't mean him to see. *Here's where he gets mad and tells me to get out.* He glanced at his watch. *Damn, past noon. I gotta get out and get busy —*

"Tell you what." Boxer relaxed and fine-tuned his smile. "Why'nchu just put fifty of that in your pocket and we play another hand with that loose five you came in here with?"

Mort looked over at him, really confused now.

"Ted," Boxer said. He nodded at the grey-haired man, but kept his eyes on Mort, nailing him down in his seat. "Tell Lola fix us some sandwiches and draw a couple beers. Might as well relax and get sociable now while I try to get a little piece of me back off old Mort here. Whattaya say there, high-roller? Just another couple hands? Just enough till I win that five off you?"

Mort hesitated.

Chapter 16
Ninety Minutes After the Robbery

December 20, 1951
11:30 AM
Slimmy

Slimmy sat in the warm station wagon, watching the landscape around him get whiter and whiter, listening to

...that glorrriouss so-ong of old,
From an-gels benn-ding near to earth,
To touch their haaaaarps of gold,
Peace onnnnn the Earrth....

He took another sip from his flask.
Damn, he thought. *Ain't they never getting here?*
He flipped around the dial on the radio with clumsy, fumbling fingers, looking for news. Any news. But all he could find was

...Two turtle doves,
Three French hens,
And a parrrtridddge....

He turned it down and took another drink. A longer one this time.

Hell, they probably botched it all to Kingdom Come, he reflected. *Leaving me out here to sit and rot. That'd probably tickle Brother Sweetie plumb to sweet mother of Jesus, leave me out here to sit and rot. Work me all day and then just put me out in the snow to sit and rot....*

He looked at the bottle and noted morosely that only about a quarter of it remained. *Well, how the hell'd that happen? Damn near gone. Out here to sit and rot and now the booze, it's damn near gone. Where are those bastards, anyhow?*

He took another drink, then tilted the bottle and looked at the tiny bit puddling sadly in one corner. *One thing,* he thought, *those bastards show up, they're gonna have to drive. Can't work me all morning and put me out here to sit and rot and then expect me to drive, too. I can't be the brains of this outfit and doing all the work, too. Nossir, they show up, I'm just going to say, "You gentlemen will have to drive, because I've been put out here to sit and—"*

A sound came from just behind him at the driver's window, a tapping. It wasn't loud, but the sudden, sharp sound of it made Slimmy lurch and drop the bottle in his lap. He looked at the trickle of liquor soaking into his pants, and it made him sad, somehow.

The tapping came again. It was like something hard and metallic on the window, just behind him. *Oh yeah,* he thought, *must be them…*

He opened the door and the weight of it or the wind or someone pulling from outside overbalanced him and sent him sliding out and into the snow. The sudden cold got his attention but it didn't sober him up. He peered up, confused, at the man who had tapped on his window.

The man wore a blue uniform and a hard look, and they both fit him pretty well. Slimmy had never seen his face before, but he was all too familiar with the look on it.

"May I see your license, sir?" the cop asked him.

Chapter 17
Three Hours and Twenty-Five Minutes
After the Robbery

December 20, 1951
12:25 PM
Officer Drapp

"But I do beg your pardon." She said it like she'd spilled tea on a laid-out doily. "I seem to have been going on about myself."

On the other side of the windshield, the snow was still beating us to death, and gusts of wind hit the square sides of that Jeep till it rocked. I had on big leather gloves with knit-wool glove liners under them, and the leather strained across my knuckles, I was clutching the wheel that tight as we moved maybe fifteen miles an hour along the park road. The tracks of the getaway car had faded into the snow, but I told myself I didn't need tracks now; there was only one way through the park and we were on it.

"That's okay." You learn that you get a person talking, they'll sooner or later get around to what you need to find out. So I tried not to clench my teeth when I said it. "Sounds like you've had an interesting time."

Well I'd got her to talking all right.

Or maybe she just got lonely sometimes, working out in the woods like that. Whatever it was, in the last half-hour I'd heard all about the life and times of Calpurnia Nixon. How her dad owned umpty-ump acres of forest out west where she used to play. Then college at some place called Barnard, but they didn't have the kind of courses she wanted, so she spent summers working at parks and lumber camps—I tried to figure what she'd be doing in a lumber camp, but nothing pretty came to mind. And then when the war came and able-bodied men were scarce, she'd got a hitch as a sure-enough Park Ranger.

"That's when I knew this was my life," she said. "Those years living in the park and looking after the woods. It seemed as if I were supposed to be here."

She paused, like she was swallowing something hard. Or maybe just stopped to take a breath, then went on. "But after the war they didn't see much need for women to be park rangers anymore."

"They fired you?"

"Colonel Powell—he was my commanding officer at the time—was quite straightforward about it," she said. "He said now the men were coming back for the jobs, well, I was taking a job away from a man who needed it and it was time I got married and raised a family." She made that noise again, like she was swallowing something hard just thinking about it. "Well, I had no plans for anything like that and I told him as much, and I'm afraid I may have been a bit vituperative. At any rate, he insisted I had to go, and that's when I found that having a cousin in politics wasn't such a bad thing."

"Yeah, I guess not." Funny, her voice was kind of pretty, and listening to her talk was almost restful. Just about took my mind off what was really going on here, and the way it was, driving in the snow and wind like this. Just listening to her helped ease the strain.

But she still hadn't got around to what I wanted to hear about.

"So with my Cousin Richard's help, I stayed in the National Parks," she said, "but they have ways of getting back at one…" She stopped talking. Just trailed off like when you pull the plug on a record player. And I needed her talking.

"Seems to me you done a pretty good job here." I tried to

sound like all those trees covered up in snow was something real special just to look at.

"Well, it's a work in progress," she said.

"What's that mean?"

"A park, a forest, is a work in progress. It keeps growing and changing—that is, if it's managed properly—and it never stops. That's the wonder of it."

"I think I see what you mean."

Actually, only thing I saw was more trees and more snow, but I figured now I'd got her relaxed, it was time to find out what it was she'd been shying away from saying since I'd met up with her. Time to use those careful, subtle questioning cop techniques you see in the movies.

"What is it you're not telling me?" I said.

"I beg your pardon?"

"There's something about this situation with your Captain out at the watchtower, and you've been dancing around it this last half-hour. Now, was there something you don't want to say, that's fine, but I get to thinking maybe we're driving into something I ought to know about, and if there is, well…maybe you ought to come out with it."

"You're probably correct." The tone in her voice sounded like she really wanted to come out with it. "But first I wonder if you could satisfy my curiosity?"

"About what?"

"How does a police officer happen to be driving around in a pick-up truck full of hay bales?" she asked. "And back at the ranger station, why didn't you call for more officers?"

"That's easy," I said, trying to think of an answer.

Chapter 18
Thirty Minutes After the Robbery

December 20, 1951
9:30 AM
Walter and Eddie

As the car that looked a little like a police car went through another patch of woods, the drifts eased up, the driving got better, and Walter felt he ought to speak what was on his mind.

"You think he meant that?" he said suddenly.

"Who meant what, do I think?"

"You think that guard, the dumb one, meant what he said about them losing their jobs because of this? Because we robbed them?"

"Hell, no." Eddie moved around on the seat, still trying to get comfortable in the long, heavy police coat and still not getting there. "Guy takes a wound like that protecting somebody else's money, he's a hero."

"You think that?"

"Sure. Guy gets his ear shot off, how's it gonna look do they fire him for it?"

"That'd be a damn shame, getting fired right at Christmas." Walter gripped the wheel a little tighter as they passed a plowed field and the wind coming across it tried to whip the car broadside, then eased a little as the road cut through a strip of woods.

"Well, I don't figure them to fire either one of those guards. One of them gets shot up and the other one puts bandages on him and saves his life…they'll be heroes and get their pictures in the papers is what'll happen. And maybe someday they'll make a movie about Vincent Van Gogh, and that dumb guard, he'll play the lead."

"Movie about who?"

"Vincent Van Gogh." Eddie watched the woods grow thicker around them again, hoping it would keep some of the falling snow off the road, or maybe just keep it from drifting as much.

"Who's Vincent Van Gogh?"

"He was a painter. He painted pictures, I mean. He was French or something, and he lived a hundred years back maybe, long time back in the days like you see in movies when everybody wrote with feathers."

"And what about him?"

"Well, he only had one ear."

"No kidding? Born like that with just one ear?"

"Naah." Eddie decided the woods weren't helping much. "He fell hard for some gal and I guess she always got mad at him or something because everybody thought his paintings stunk, so one time when she got mad at him, he cut off his ear and sent it to her to show her he was sorry."

"Damn! No joke?"

"No joke."

"He cut off his ear?"

"Yep."

"And sends it to his girlfriend?"

"That's what he done. Just to show he was sorry."

"Damn."

"I couldn't say it better myself."

"He must of been awful sorry."

"Well, that's how come he to have only one ear, and I figure maybe sometime they'll make a movie about him and start looking around for actors who got just one ear, and then they don't find any so they come to this guy and they make him a big movie star or something."

"Yeah." Walter studied the road ahead and shifted hands on the steering wheel. "How come you to know about this Vincent Van Gogh?"

"That stretch I did give me plenty of time to read."

"I guess so." Walter sounded awkward about bringing it up.

"It wasn't so bad, I guess." Eddie sounded unconvinced by his own words. "I read a lot and learned card tricks—"

"You can do card tricks?"

"It ain't hard. Like selling something. Mostly it's getting the other guy to look where you want him to look. And like I say, I got to read a lot of stuff I wouldn't have otherwise."

"My brother," Walter said, "he was a big one for reading."

"Yeah?"

"Oh yeah." Walter crawled the heavy car around a gentle curve, easing the clutch in and out, moving the gearshift up and back with the efficiency of long practice. "Most of us, if we got a book some way, we just used it for toilet paper or to roll cigarettes, but my brother, he loved to read."

"That's the one you're going to visit?"

"Going to visit his wife. And the kids. He dead."

"That's right." Eddie tried to sound solemn talking about the dead. "You said it was a long time back?"

"Few years back," Walter said tonelessly. "They burned him up."

"Burned him up? He burned to death, your brother?"

"They burned him," Walter repeated. "Kids out of high school or not much older. Used to tear around the county that summer, making wild, driving reckless up and down the back roads, just going crazy 'cause they wasn't in school no more, and making trouble."

"And they set fire to your brother?"

"He hadn't done nothing. And nobody ever said for sure they did it. It was just they had the chance, and I guess they wanted to see how it felt like to do a thing like that. Like they'd heard about folks doing back in the day."

"They go to jail for it?" Eddie knew the answer already but he asked anyway. "Anybody ever arrest them?"

"Nobody never tried," Walter said patiently. "His wife, she talked to the sheriff and the chief of police, but nobody took them to law. Never got the chance, maybe they would have, but it didn't look like they was going to."

"Never got the chance?"

"Those boys, they got cracked up in that car of theirs. They used to go tearing up and down the same old back roads late at night, like I said, and one night they run smack into a car somebody had stole and left it over a hill where they couldn't see it till too late to stop. Run smack into it. Catch fire, sure did."

"Killed them all?" Again, Eddie thought he knew the answer.

"None of them lived," Walter said simply.

"Nice work."

"Yeah, but I had to beat feet out of there, and sudden, too. Would've liked to take my brother's wife and the kids with me, but no time for that."

"That's when you come North?"

"And ended up working for Brother Sweetie, yeah."

"Probably better for a black man up here anyway."

"You reckon like that?" Walter worked the clutch again, on a sharper curve this time, and both men held their breath as the rear wheels slid, then bit back at the snow, regaining control.

Eddie gave a silent sigh of relief. Then,

"You mean it ain't?" he asked. "It ain't any easier for a black man up here than down South?"

"It's different, some, but—" Walter squinted, and Eddie

couldn't tell if he was groping for the right words or just trying to see better through the pummeling snow. "Well, it's like down South they got signs up, Whites Only, No Blacks Allowed. Like that. I don't read maybe, but I learn to know those signs quick enough. They got places a black man don't go and they say it plain. Up here, they don't got the signs maybe, but they got the same places where a black man don't go, and they got ways of saying it. Just different, that's all. And no signs. You got to just look at a place and try to figure if—"

He stopped. Stared straight ahead.

From the side of the road, a massive, grey-brown buck with antlers like a hat rack rose up from cover that couldn't have hid a rabbit and walked out into the road in front of them.

And then just stood there in front of the oncoming car.

"Oh hell. Hell!" Walter slammed in the clutch, fanned the brakes and spun the wheel. The heavy car slid sideways, crossways, backwards, and past the buck, who gave it a wide-eyed stare and disappeared again.

"Damn, Eddie, I'm sorry!" Walter just had time to shout it as the car kept sliding in slow motion, off the road and into a drain-ditch.

Chapter 19
Three Hours and Fifteen Minutes
After the Robbery

December 20, 1951
12:15 PM
Slimmy and the Cop

Slimmy sat in the back of the patrol car, contemplating his tragic fate and reflecting on the unfairness of life in general.

"Snot fair," he sniffed.

The officer in front concentrated on driving in the heavy snow, and thus missed his chance for a philosophical discussion on the meaning of it all.

"Snot fair!" Slimmy yelled, prompting the officer to enter the debate.

"Quiet back there, I gotta drive in this crap."

"You can't arrest me."

"Oh."

"You can't arrest me 'cause I wasn't driving, ya stupid son of a—" Slimmy stopped himself before he said something plumb-dumb.

The officer appreciated it. "I'm not arresting you for *driving* drunk," he said patiently. "There's a law against being in control of a motor vehicle when you're drunk; that's what I'm arresting you for. I told you that already. Twice."

"But I wasn't driving!" Slimmy told himself he'd run rings around the officer's logic, but saw it wasn't getting him anywhere, so he tried another approach to the question at hand.

"Well, they left me to sit and rot." He looked around the tiny back seat of the patrol car and tried to remember the point he was trying to make. "And now, they just going to leave me to sit and rot some more!"

"You don't have to yell about it." Something was coming over the radio and the officer strained to hear it.

"But you don't get it, you don't understand it." Now Slimmy felt he'd touched a kindred spirit, one who could see the unfairness of his life. "Those guys, they rob folks! They lie and they cheatya and they rob and then... " What was he thinking? Oh yeah— "They rob and they—they're all gonna get off scot-free! And I'm just gonna sit and rot! They're the ones who rob and take stuff, and the only one going to jail is me, dammit! And they done the robbing!"

"I said quiet." The officer pulled off the snowy road as much as he dared and reached under the dashboard to turn up the radio. Listened close, trying to shut out the whining from the back seat.

"...any car in the vicinity of Highway 12 and the Willisburg Cut-off," the tinny voice repeated, "come in, please. Any car in the vicinity of Highway 12 and the Willisburg Cut-off—come in. Over."

"Car Three-Six," he keyed the mike, "I'm close to Piketon Point and Highway 12. Over."

"Car Three-Six," the voice inside the radio came back at him, "sounds like you're the closest. Need you to check the Willisburg Cut-off. The Ajax Truck didn't show up on time. Over."

Behind him, he heard wicked laughter.

"Car Three-Six," he said into the mike, "I'm not surprised they're running late in this snow—"

"Running late?" the booze-soaked voice behind him sneered. "They ain't never going to get to Willisburg, mister!"

"Maybe they ran off the road or something." The officer

tried to tune out the drunk in the back and concentrate. "Haven't they called in? Over."

"No they ain't called in." Slimmy for once in his life felt smug and superior to the dumb cop who just happened, he reasoned, by some quirk of fate, to have him handcuffed in the back of a car. "And they ain't going to call! I know all about that Ajax Truck, mister, and they ain't never going to get there at all!"

"…Chief wants it checked," the radio was saying, "and it sounds like you're the only one close. Over."

"I got a D–D in here in the back," the officer argued, "I was just bringing him in. Over."

"Bringing me in," Slimmy added his opinion from the back, "and letting those bastards go! When they done the robbing and then left me to sit and rot!"

A new voice came over the radio. One used to being obeyed. "Listen up, Three–Six." It was Chief Hannon himself. "We know it's snowing here; we're not blind. Get rid of the D-D and get to looking for the Ajax Truck. Do you read me? Over."

The voice from the back seat kept yammering: "I can tell you all about that truck, and it ain't never getting to Willisburg…" But the officer driving had just heard the word of God, or something close to it, and he wasn't listening to anything else.

"Yessir," he said quickly. "Over and out."

Chapter 20
The Getaway

"Looks like we got us a job of work getting out of here." Walter felt the snow turn his pants legs cold and wet as he stood outside and looked down at the car in the ditch. The two passenger-side wheels were sunk deep and the front driver-side wheel damn near as much, but they still had one back wheel over the road. Walter studied it, then peered into the woods around them. "Ain't gonna be easy, though. Let's find us a tree."

Standing next to Walter, blowing on his gloved hands for warmth, Eddie looked at the woods around them too. "Should be a tree around here someplace," he said. "Which one you want?"

"We want us a dead-fallen tree." Walter walked the wood-line at the edge of the road, legs sinking nearly knee-deep into the snow as he peered into the bare edge of the forest. "Dead but not rotted. Long but not too heavy. And not a lot of big branches on it—too hard to move."

They left the road and plodded into the woods.

"I can't say it enough," Walter said again, "I'm sorry, Eddie. I shoulda just run right into that damn animal. It was automatic, you know, just to hit the brakes and spin out like that."

"Times like that your feet do the thinking," Eddie said, "I'd of done it myself."

"But you wasn't driving. I was, and I'm sorry."

"Well don't go cutting off your ear or nothing. You likely done the right thing anyhow."

"You figure that's facts?"

"I figure did you hit that big buck head-on you might of cracked the radiator and that would of stopped us sure. This way all you done was to put us in a ditch."

"And I've had me some practice how to get out of a ditch." Walter stopped at a fallen tree and looked it over. "Let's us try this one."

It had a smooth trunk. Eddie didn't know what kind of tree, but the bark had long since fallen away, leaving a hardwood pole less than a foot thick and maybe twenty feet long. He pulled one end out of an overgrown thicket while Walter lifted the other half.

"Back to the work fields." Walter steered them through the woods back to the road, lurching awkwardly through the snow and underbrush as Eddie tried to match his pace. Both men were breathing hard by the time they reached the car. Without a word, Walter steered them to the front of the car and jammed the tree as far as he could under the bumper, where it rested on the edge of the ditch.

"Okay, lift!"

They threw their shoulders into it, lifted for all they were worth.

The front of the car came up level with the roadway.

"Up higher…"

Walter put the tree over his shoulder and strained. The bumper moved higher, almost clear of the snow.

"Now over!"

They levered toward the road, and the car moved almost out of the ditch.

Then the tree broke.

Walter looked at it.

"Find us another." He panted as more snow blew into his face.

Eddie looked at the broken tree, sighed and followed Walter into the woods.

"Damn, that was a lot like work." Walter steered the car through a straight stretch of snow-drifted road, listening to the tire chains clank against the icy roadway.

"Pretty close." Eddie lit another cigarette, drew in a deep lungful, then passed it over to Walter and held it to his lips. "How's she driving?"

"Don't feel like we bent a rod or nothing." Walter inhaled deeply off the cigarette and adjusted his hands on the steering wheel.

Eddie brought the cigarette back and took another lungful of smoke. "Where'd you learn to move a car out of a ditch like that?"

"Back home," Walter said. "I grew up out in the middle of no place. And I'm here to tell you it was damn smack spang right in the middle of no place, too. Or maybe you'd get to the middle of no place and us folks we lived in the next holler back of there. Nearest store with a phone and electric was two miles to walk there, and nobody 'round us had money to buy nothing nohow."

"So you had to do for yourself?"

"We done for ourself and then some. Getting cars out from a mud-wallow was just one little part of it."

"No wonder you up and went to the city."

"Yeah." Walter made a short laugh-sound. "But if I'd have knowed about this snow, I mighta just stayed back down there in the mud-wallows."

"I'm starting to see the wisdom there." Eddie stared out at the sheet of white coldness all around them as the car moved fitfully through the soggy mess. "But I'm real happy-glad you got that trick of getting a car out of a ditch. I've towed my share of cars out of plenty ditches myself, but I always had a truck or something to do it with."

"You used to pull cars out from ditches?" Walter asked.

"Not me personal, not if I could help it. Jeeps mostly. And trucks of course. It's what I did in the war." Eddie took another deep drag off the cigarette. "I got trucks, Jeeps and wheels out of ditches for the 101st Airborne and fixed whatever those guys had brains enough not to break beyond fixing." He looked out the window. The woods had given way to another farmer's field, and the snow drifts ran deeper where wind crossed the road.

"I told you I worked in the motor pool," he went on. "Got that job because I figured fixing engines was safer than shooting Germans. Only it seemed like was there a ditch, a crater, a creek or a canyon fifty miles in any direction from this man's army, some GI he'd drive right into it. Where I was, mostly there was a truck handy someplace or even a tank to pull it out. Or maybe five or six GIs with strong backs and a nasty non-com, so we could make it up as we went along. And one thing they had plenty handy in that man's war was GIs and nasty non-coms."

"You was in the motor pool all through the war, then?"

"Yup. Seemed pretty soft and pretty safe till one winter morning when they got all us guys in the motor pool up out of bed, handed us rifles and marched a bunch of us out to some place near Bastogne. Some non-com put a bunch of us behind a wall at a burned-out house and said I was in charge and we was to stay there. And next thing was, every German in the world come running up the hill at us. Wasn't so nice then."

"You talking about the Battle of the Bulge? You was in that?"

"Didn't mean to be." Eddie passed the cigarette over to Walter and held it for him again, then took a last puff himself. "We figured we had 'em—the Germans, I mean—we figured we had 'em beat by then and soon as the snow cleared we'd march across the Rhine and into Berlin. No one was much thinking they'd hit us back in the middle of winter like that."

"I remember my brother reading me about that in the papers," Walter said, "Battle of the Bulge. And you was there."

"Not like I planned on it or nothing." Eddie stubbed the cigarette out in the overflowing ashtray, watching the empty fields crawl past outside. "I hadn't shot a rifle since boot camp. Hell, I'd of turned and got out of there, only it was safer to squat down and shoot."

"You stopped the Germans?"

"We slowed them up some I guess, us grease monkeys and typists there behind that wall. It gets into you some way and you keep shooting. Go crazy maybe and just keep shooting. Anyhow the line held in our sector and I got stuck there in a trench for days and nights no end, firing whatever I got my hands on. Didn't like it much."

"Damn." Walter almost smiled. "I got me a war hero for a partner."

"You'll have you a war hero for a cellmate do they catch up to us."

"You figure they behind us? Or ahead of us?"

"I figure like this," Eddie said. "Did everything break our way, they haven't even found the truck yet."

"Luck's a chance, but trouble's sure."

"What's that mean?"

"Just something my brother read to me once," Walter said. "My brother, the one that's dead, he used to read us poems, and some I remember: 'Luck's a chance, but trouble's sure.' "

"He got that right." Eddie looked thoughtful. "But even did they find that truck, and they got the story on us, they're still some ways behind."

"Not in front? You thinking about roadblocks?"

"They can't get any roadblocks anywhere in front of us, weather like this. And I don't think they'll figure us to cut through the park. Brother Sweeetie's bright idea. Anyone sets up roadblocks they won't be there."

"That's likely."

"Yeah, but did they get behind us, they could be moving up. Hard to miss tire tracks come through the snow like this, and they might have a Jeep or something to make better time. And that hour we spent in the ditch didn't help us none."

"I'm damn sorry about that."

"Not your fault." Eddie looked out his window. "But one thing sure: we get caught, Brother Sweetie ain't going to blame some deer."

"Yeah, we lose this money, we gonna look awful short next to him."

"He'll nail our ass to the wall, is what he'll do."

Walter thought a minute. "But if maybe they're behind us, I know a way to stop them." At a patch of road by a culvert the snow had drifted away to just a couple inches deep, and he eased in the clutch and let the car roll to a stop.

"Farmhouse out there." He nodded toward a vague shape through the blowing snow. "And like as not they got them a truck parked in a barn someplace."

"Like as not," Eddie said. "What you thinking?"

"I'm gonna get out here and steal me a truck. Should be easy enough, and the big wheels on a heavy truck will get me through over roads like this."

"Yeah they will, but I still don't know what you're thinking."

"I'm thinking you drive this car on ahead and I get me that truck and follow you behind. Don't wait for me or nothing. We ain't got the kind of time you should wait for me. Just let me out here and you drive and keep going to the meeting place.

And I'll be someways behind you in the truck. That way, you get stuck or go off the road again, I come up behind and we load the money in the truck and keep going. And here's the other part: if someone *is* following us, and he come up behind me, I can make like I'm in an accident and block the road."

"So I get through to the rendezvous?"

"That's the idea. It comes down to it, I'll just play like I'm dumb. Things get tight, I can take off on foot. Even if they catch me, all they got me on is stealing a truck."

"Walter, you got brains, you have."

"Thank you, Eddie."

"Only it ain't going to work."

"You figure not?"

"I figure is there anyone in that farmhouse, and likely there is, I figure they see you coming through the snow and heading to that truck, well, some farmer's going to come out with his shotgun, and next spring he'll point out your head hanging over his fireplace."

"I can handle any farmer."

"But you don't got to," Eddie said. "I can steal the truck easy."

"You figure so?"

"I figure I'm dressed like a cop," Eddie said, "And does any farmer come out with his shotgun, most likely I can talk my way around it. And a farmer's not gonna be so quick to shoot a cop as a—" He swallowed the word he was about to say.

"Could be."

"Gotta be." Eddie put a hand on the door handle. "So we do it just like you said, only you drive off and I come up behind in that truck. Got it?"

"Eddie," Walter said slowly, "you're a good man to be with on a job like this."

"You say so." Eddie opened the door. And gasped as the sharp, cold wind bit into his face. "But I'm working awful hard for a living these days." He got out fast, like a swimmer plunging into cold water.

"Just keep going," he shouted into the car, "I'll either come up behind you or block the trail."

"Good luck, buddy."

"Ain't no such thing on a job like this." Eddie slammed the door shut and began wading through knee-deep snow toward the farmhouse.

And the truck.

Chapter 21
Three Hours and Forty-Five Minutes
After the Robbery

December 20, 1951
12:45 PM
Officer Drapp

And there I was, pushing that Jeep through all the snow in the world and trying to figure out how to tell that ranger-lady how I come to be driving a farm truck up to her station earlier on.

"I'm trying to figure out how to tell it," I said. "You ever met Chief Hannon?"

"Is that your boss?" she inquired politely, "Chief Hannon? You work for him?"

"For him or against him," I said. "And I'm trying to think how to tell about him, the kind of guy he is. You don't know him, he's hard to tell about. You ever meet the man?"

"I don't believe I've had that privilege, no."

"Well then it's hard to tell about him. Lemme see…. You ever buy a bag of peanuts?"

"I'm sure I have." I saw her raising an eyebrow. It wasn't dainty.

"Well on every bag of peanuts there's this picture of a guy and he's Mr. Peanut. You know who I mean?"

"You mean the peanut?"

"Yeah, he's a peanut, yeah, but he's not just any peanut, he's *Mister Peanut*, you know? He's six foot tall and he's some snazzy dresser and he comes strutting down the street with his top hat and that looking-glass in his eye, swinging a cane, and it's like he's the greatest peanut in the world, king of the peanuts or something; he's not your ordinary peanut: he's Mister Peanut to you—you know how I mean?"

"He's Mister Peanut, yes?"

"That's it. And Chief Hannon, he's Mister Ass—uh—Mister Armpit."

"I'd swear you were about to say something off-color." But it got a laugh out of her. Sounded something like a cross between a little silver bell tinkling in the rain and the noise a mule makes when you kick it, but I was glad I got it because it meant she was relaxing, and you get more answers from them when they're off guard.

Up ahead, what used to be the tire tracks I was following were now just marks in the snow, but they were still easy to read. And when I took my eyes off the road for half a split second I could just see the top of the fire tower—where this Captain Scranton guy was supposed to be for some reason on a day like this—through the bare branches of the trees and the blowing white mess up above.

"The thing is this," I said. "When something big comes over like this, Chief Hannon he wants everybody to do like he says, and just that: nothing else but what he says. I guess maybe was I running things maybe I'd want that too. But Chief Hannon he doesn't want you figuring nothing out on your own. If he didn't think of it, well it's not a good idea. And say you try to come up with something just yourself, he can't have it, see?"

"I think so; I think I've worked for men like that." She said *men* like it was a dirty word, but I guess she'd got a fair amount of trouble working with men—or trying to work with them. Me, I been a man most of my life. I started out as a little kid, like everybody else, but I been a man most of my life now, and I worked and lived with men in the Army—it was pretty much all men in the Army back then—and I never had a high opinion of us myself, so I could see why she said it like that.

"So when this armored car doesn't show up on time, word comes out from Chief Hannon, he says do a roadblock at the edge of town there, then start working out, looking for the truck. And I'm the roadblock and that's way out, just a couple miles maybe from the park here, only when I get out here I get word on the radio there's a farmhouse not far from me, and the farmer says some guy there tried to steal his truck and he caught him doing it and he's holding him at the end of a shotgun."

"My goodness!"

"Yeah, that's just what I said—something like that anyway." I took the Jeep around a curve in the trail past the trees to a clearing and almost all of the fire tower came into view at the top of a rise, like some big tall metal-monster-giant standing up and facing into the snow. I shifted the Jeep into a lower gear and steadied the wheel to move up that rise as I talked.

"So I get on the radio and I tell the chief I ought to go check this out because it might be it's got something to do with our missing armored car full of money. But he says I should just sit there on the roadblock and wait for someone to come along because that farmhouse it's outside the city and he don't want to bother with it."

"But you thought you should?"

"Yeah, and I did more than think it. I drove over there and took a look and dam—uh—darned but this guy the farmer caught, he looks like one of our robbers."

"You knew what they looked like?"

"Yeah, by then they found the armored car and got us a description, and this guy was one of them, but I could see tracks in the snow where the other one had drove off with the money."

"How did you know he drove off with the money?"

"Pardon?"

"You said the other one drove off with the money. How do you know if you didn't see him?"

"Tracks in the snow," I said.

"What do you mean?"

"Time I got there, you could still see tracks in the snow." I spelled it out to her. "And there weren't any looked like somebody dragged big bags of money. Besides which, there wasn't any money there."

Up ahead, the track of the getaway car still rolled out in front of me—but now there was something funny about it. Couldn't tell what, in all that snow, but…

"They split up?" Callie interrupted my squinting at those tracks. She must have thought my story was getting interesting now. "Why on earth did they do such a thing?"

"Well, this guy the farmer caught, he didn't feel like talking about it much." I tried to keep part of my mind on telling her this and part on figuring out those tracks. It was like I could see them going up halfway to the tower but no further. The tracks just stopped, but there was no car there.

And I kept talking: "But I knew was I to get after his partner I had to move out quick, and I also knew I wasn't going to make it very far or very fast in the car I was driving. But there was that truck."

"The truck he got caught trying to steal?"

"Right. There was that truck and it was a darn sight better for getting over roads like these. 'Most as good as this Jeep."

I could see it for sure now. We were maybe a quarter-mile from the tower and it was like driving up to big giant legs. There was some kind of small Park Service truck setting under it, and whatever tracks it made getting there had been long-ago covered in snow. But I could see pretty clear the tracks I'd been following, and they didn't go no further than maybe forty yards up from the tower.

Callie acted like she didn't notice it, and maybe she didn't.

"Perhaps that's why your man got out and tried to steal it," she said, "and then when he got caught his partner simply drove away with the money."

"Likely that or something just close to it." I slowed up. We were close enough to the tower now that I couldn't see the top of it through the windshield, but I wasn't looking at it anyway. I was trying to see where those tracks in the snow had gone. "Anyhow, I handcuffed our man to a radiator, got the farmer to loan me his truck—"

"And showed up on my doorstep."

"And couldn't call for help because Chief Hannon, he didn't suppose I ought to be there to start with."

She was ready to talk. Driving in that snow I couldn't take time to look at her face, but I could tell it anyway. Feel it just from the tone of her voice and the air in that Jeep.

"So now," I said. "What's your story about this Captain Scranton?"

And then I saw them; saw the tracks, saw where they went.

That little rise we'd been climbing to where the tower sat, it had a sharp drop-off to our left. And now that we were right up on them, I could see those tracks veered off, maybe forty yards in front of the tower and went sideways down the slope.

At the bottom of that slope the snow suddenly turned flat and level for maybe a half mile, so I figured there was likely a lake down there. And right at the edge of that lake, almost covered in snow there was a black-and-white car.

And footprints.

"It looks like a police car," Callie said helpfully.

I hit the clutch and the brake, pulled up the Jeep and pressed my face up against the freezing-cold window, trying to see through blowing snow: one set of tracks, running from the passenger side of the car to the tower and back. Or maybe from the tower to the car, then back. I couldn't be sure. Tried to look closer.

Which is how we were, just sitting there, stock-still out in the open like that, when I heard a sound I'd only heard the like of once before; it only come on me one other time, back in the war, but that was too many times to mistake it for anything else.

There was that short-sharp-sudden noise and all to once the windshield of that Jeep tuned into a crystal-white spiderweb with a big nasty hole in the middle of it.

Chapter 22
Three Hours and Fifty-Five Minutes
After the Robbery

December 20, 1951
12:55 PM
Sarge

At Sarge's Spot, the only business for two miles in either direction out on Highway 12, Sarge himself looked disgustedly around the soft-lit polished-plastic room full of empty booths and tables, the only noise there coming from the flashing red-and-yellow jukebox,

Sleeeep in heavvvvenly peee-eeece,
Slee-eep in heavvvv-enly peace.

"You got that right," he muttered to himself, took off his spotless white apron and walked to the big glass door leading to the gravel parking lot out front.

Nothing there but snow. White, deep, and unbroken by any tire tracks all day.

"Hell," he said to nobody but himself.

Behind him, Joe opened the door from the kitchen and looked timidly out.

"You want I should pitch this coffee and make some fresh, Boss?"

"Nah." Sarge couldn't take his eyes off the empty, money-losing parking lot. "Ain't nobody gonna come out in a mess like this." He reached up to turn off the bright blue-white-and-gold sign outside with the three stripes and the big letters

SARGE'S

SPOT

Dining – Dancing – Good Food

Beer –Wine – Liquor

He wondered vaguely if he'd make enough yet this year to pay off Brother Sweetie and get clear. Maybe if he got a good crowd on Christmas Eve...and then New Year's.... Yeah, he could count on a good crowd New Year's Eve, and Sweeney wouldn't expect to get paid right away anyhow, not right around the holidays like this, so if things broke right, he might make it. With a little luck and a good crowd. Not today, though. Nor tonight either. Might as well—

Something out there caught his eye. Some kind of car, big and black, coming up Highway 12 as fast as it could on a day like this. Sarge tightened his fingers on the light switch. *Just one car,* he thought, *and if they decide to stop and get out of this mess they might sit here for hours waiting for the snow plow to come by, just sitting here drinking coffee and using up my electricity....*

He almost turned off the switch. Then he reflected that whoever was out there might really need a chance to stop and rest. Might want something hot. Maybe need it bad, out there driving in all this. He listened a moment to the sentimental music coming from the jukebox and figured he might as well wait and see if whoever it was stopped in. Just for Christmas' sake.

Sure enough, the car slowed as it got closer and Sarge swore softly to himself. *A damn cop car. All I'm going to get out of this is some damn cop wants a free cup of coffee and take a leak, using up my water....*

He paused. Funny, the car didn't really park out front. Not like the cop inside wanted to come in. He just pulled up fast, sliding in the snow right up to the door, and jumped out as soon as it stopped.

Sarge watched with growing interest as the cop went to the driver-side back door, hunkering down in the pelting snow like a boxer in the ring, and pulled out some guy in handcuffs. Took off the cuffs, turned the guy toward Sarge's big glass door and gave him a gentle push that sent him reeling toward the building. By the time the man outside got his balance the cop was already back in the car, spinning his wheels in the snow and moving back out onto Highway 12.

Sarge watched him depart, then turned his attention to the discharged passenger. *Damn, it's Slimmy Johnson out there! What's he doing clear out —*

Sarge looked closer. What Slimmy was doing was relieving himself against the wall by the door.

He flipped off the switch for the electric sign outside, wondering how he was going to get rid of him. Couldn't just leave him out in the snow; even a pill like Slimmy Johnson you couldn't leave out on a day like this. "But I sure as hell ain't gonna keep him here long," Sarge muttered. He wondered how Slimmy come to ride up to his door in a black-and-white taxi. Sarge figured there maybe was an interesting story here, and he put on his best professional smile as Slimmy finally got his bearings and reeled through the door saying, "Hey, where can a man get a drink around here?"

Chapter 23
Three Hours and Fifty-Eight Minutes
After the Robbery

December 20, 1951
12:58 PM
Officer Drapp

"We're under fire!" Callie yelled.

Which was thoughtful of her, I guess, but I didn't need her right there with the news. I was already rolling out the door into the snow, trying to keep as much of that Jeep body between me and the tower as I could while I fast-crawled to the back.

That's where I ran into Callie again. Didn't know a big woman like her could move so fast, but then she looked a little surprised to see me there too.

We were both hunkered down in the snow, hugging the back of that Jeep like a baby getting mama's milk, just staring at each other.

I got to say she handled it all right. Most folks, they don't much care to get shot at, and it shakes them up some, but she just had this look on her face like this was a job of work now, but she wasn't going to let it scare her much.

Me, I was scared.

I mean, there we were, sitting in the snow back of that Jeep and the only thing warm was the fumes coming from out the tailpipe. Somewhere in the back of my head I was glad I'd put the gearshift in neutral before we jumped out, and I remembered I'd pulled the parking brake automatically—another good habit the Army taught me—so the Jeep wasn't going to roll away from us any.

But this was still a damn mess, and we were in it.

Callie sat close down beside me and got her legs up like I had, both of us hoping we weren't leaving anything out for whoever was in that tower to take a bead on. "Looks like your bank robber got here ahead of us."

All I said was, "Somebody did."

"You mean that police car?" Inside the big fur hood she moved her head towards the slope to one side of us. "Another officer got here ahead of us?"

"I don't see how," I said. "We've only been following one set of tracks."

"Well obviously your bank robber got up in the tower some-how and started shooting at us. Perhaps he even shot at the police car. Isn't that what you think?"

"Doesn't figure." I rolled carefully to one side, keeping the Jeep between me and the tower, and looked down the slope at the black-and-white car that was already getting lost in the falling snow. I rolled back.

"Those footprints. You saw them?" I asked.

"Between the car and the tower?"

"Yeah. You got a look at them?"

"A short look, yes."

"I'm no woodsman," I said, "but the way I read those tracks, whoever it was just made one round trip. One trip to and one trip from."

Somewhere inside that Eskimo hood, she caught on, and her eyes narrowed. "Let me see that."

Then all over sudden she was rolling on me like one of those heavyweight wrestlers you see on TV, like the Iron Russian or Two-Ton Frank or somebody like that, trying to get a look at those tracks without making a target of herself. Reminded me of once when I was a kid I got sat on by a horse, only this didn't have that rosy afterglow. She sprawled across me, squinting into the snow, studying the footprints best she could, her breath making heavy steam in the cold air, then she rolled back off me, praise God.

"I can't be certain." She pulled her eyebrows together—it was to help her think, I guess, but it made her face look like a clenched fist. "There's been a great deal of snow, and whoever made those tracks walked back in his own footprints."

"Another thing," I said. "Those tracks are at the passenger side of the car, closest to the tower."

"I don't see your point, I'm afraid."

"Did someone get out of the car and went to the tower, they would most likely have used the driver-side. But did someone go from the tower to the car…"

"…they would have gone straight to the passenger side, which is closer," she finished. "My, you *are* a detective, aren't you?"

"Don't need to be a detective to tell where those shots came from," I said.

"So it's your conclusion that someone went from the tower to the car, then back."

"Where they took a shot at us, whoever it was."

"Officer Drapp, I'm getting a terrible suspicion…"

"And I'm thinking maybe you better tell me about this Captain Scranton." I hugged my coat a little tighter around me. "And do it quick."

She thought on that a second. Then something inside her relaxed and let it come pouring out, what she'd been trying not to tell me.

"Well, they have ways of getting back at one…" She said it like a sigh. "You may remember I told you that."

"Those folks that didn't think you ought to be a Park Ranger?"

I leaned back on the jerry can mounted next to the spare tire on the tailgate of the Jeep, and pulled my feet up a little closer. "Them, you mean?"

"The ones who didn't think any woman should be in a job like this." She almost snarled it. "And believe you me, there are plenty of them out there." She pushed her back against the spare tire, and I felt the Jeep sway. "So when they saw they had to keep me on, they sent me here to work with Captain Scranton; I believe they supposed he'd drive me into quitting all on my own."

"He's tough on you? Tough to get along with?"

"Like Hitler on a bad day, only not nearly so calm and rational," she said. "And not much of a ranger either, if you ask me. He frequently comes to work drunk—or so badly hung-over as makes no difference. He swears at visitors sometimes, and I rather suspect him of pilfering."

"You figure he'd shoot us over pilfering?"

"Well he also likes to hunt here."

"Didn't know could you hunt in a park like this."

"It's against the rules," she said patiently, "very clearly and plainly against the rules. And as if hunting in a nature preserve weren't bad enough, he's begun bringing in paying guests. Other hunters, I mean. Men who would pay him to hunt on the park grounds here where game is plentiful."

"Hunting in a park?" I shivered in the cold and tried to look around us, wondering about whoever was in that tower—and was he up to something else yet. "Why don't they just shoot birds in a bag?"

"Not to mention the danger presented to hikers and campers."

"So what happened?"

"I got proof of his misconduct is what happened." She rubbed her hands, trying to get the cold out of her fingers, I guess. "And I directed it to an office where I knew it would get proper attention. Things were just coming to a head, and I was of the opinion that Captain Scranton would lose his job and face criminal charges in the New Year, but…"

She'd stopped short, like it hurt to say this next part, and I didn't have time for that. Or anything like it.

"But what?"

"They redirected my charges to Captain Scranton—for him to investigate."

"How come they didn't just kill you outright?"

"I suspect that would have been an easier death." She bit out the words like this had been a hard thing for her to take. Couldn't blame her, either. If someone did me like that…well they better not let me get too close up near to them, that's all.

"Since then, he's been getting even more ill-tempered," she went on when she could, "and drinking more as well, and sometimes he'd look at me as if—" She shivered, and I didn't figure it was from the cold. "—well, it wasn't very pleasant around here lately, and we took to avoiding each other. Today he took the service truck out to the tower, and I thought he just intended to stay up there and drink himself to oblivion, but then I guess your bank robber showed up, and then that policeman—isn't that a police car?"

"Looks like one," I said, "but it just doesn't figure. I followed one set of tracks from that farmhouse to here. And you only saw one car go by, you told me."

"I didn't actually see it," she reminded me, "I merely heard it pass and saw the tracks."

"I'm just trying to think," I started.

I felt a little kick in my foot and heard a *crack*!

And all come at once I saw a fresh clean tear in the toe of my boot. I jerked it in close to me fast as I could.

"Oh my god," Callie said calmly and stared at it. "Are you hit?"

I stared at it myself, not exactly sure. Then I thought to reach out and feel around the toe. "Didn't miss it by much," I said finally. "Glad I got big shoes and thick socks."

She rolled a bit, took a quick look at the tower, then back to me. "Whoever's up there seems a proficient shot," she said.

"Seems like," I said.

"Well," she went on in a voice like she was starting spring cleaning and meant to get it done, "I suppose we shall have to find some way to get at him."

Chapter 24
Four Hours and Twelve Minutes
After the Robbery

December 20, 1951
1:12 PM
Officer Drapp

"It's not our party," I said. "It's his party, whoever's up there, and he calls the tune."

A fresh blast of wind went past us, and even in the shelter of the back of that Jeep, I could feel the cold.

"Do you think it's your robber or my captain?" Callie's teeth were starting to chatter some, and she clamped them tight.

"Whoever it is, he's too many for us," I said. "But maybe I can find out…."

I stood up behind the Jeep, took off my hat and waved my arms at whoever was in the tower.

It got close.

I just had time to see the barrel of a high-powered rifle stick out the bottom of a louvered window at the top of that tower, and I quick hit the ground again, right ahead of a shot that dinged a hole in the roof of the Jeep.

Then I was crouched down behind the Jeep again and Callie was looking at me like she wished she could quit my side and join the other team.

"Grease us twice!" she swore. "I'm sure you had some good reason for that; would you care to share it with me?"

"Whoever's up there," I said, "when they shot at us they

didn't know there was a cop inside; they just saw it was the park jeep and shot at it."

"Go on." She sounded less mad at me and more interested.

"Well, your average Joe, he thinks twice about shooting at a cop—that's my experience, anyway—so I thought…"

"You thought that if it was my captain up there and not your bank robber, he might not shoot at you?"

"Maybe he might not. Right now we got to think at getting out of here."

"Well our shooter, whoever he is, hasn't disabled the Jeep. But I rather doubt he'll let us drive it out."

"Don't seem likely." I noticed my nose was starting to sting from the cold, and I wiped snot off it with my sleeve. I looked around at the open space between us and the nearest cover, and it looked awful big and awful open. "And was we to try running off, we'd most likely get shot down or freeze to death. But we sure as Cleveland can't stay here a whole lot longer."

"An hour perhaps," she said, like she was reading out of a manual, "until hypothermia sets in and we become too weak to move."

"That quick?"

"Well, sometime before that, we'll become somewhat disoriented and apathetic as our body functions slow. That's the first stage of it. But I'd guess that we probably have twenty minutes—fifteen or twenty, let's say fifteen just to be safe—before any pronounced effect starts to set in. Have you any notion as to what we might do?"

"Well," I said and rolled over, took a mental measure and rolled right back again, "looks like maybe forty yards to the base of that tower. Through this snow, I might be able to get there in less than a minute, if I don't get shot first."

"You propose running to the tower?"

"Once one of us is underneath him—hey, is there heat up there?"

"There's an electric heater in the cab, yes."

"Cab?"

"That's what we call the little cabin at the top."

"Well, that's it then. You draw some attention by shooting up at the cab while I run to the tower and disconnect the power at the base. Then he's got to come out or freeze, and I'm guessing that up there in that wind he'll get a lot colder than us down here."

"You may be right." She seemed kind of surprised to see me do that much clear thinking, but whether it was because I was a policeman or because I was a man, period, I wasn't sure. "And once we're under the tower, we could stay warm in the truck he drove out here while he kept getting colder. But it's not your job to run to the tower; that's my job, isn't it?"

"Not like I see it, it ain't."

"It's my park." She said it like she was doing seating arrangements for a tea party. "I'm responsible for what happens here, and to some extent it may be my fault that we're in this situation. Had you known about Captain Scranton—had I told you earlier—you might have done something differently."

"Can't figure what it'd be." I sucked snot up my nose again.

"Neither can I, but that's neither here nor there." She started squirming around in that big coat of hers, like a cow giving birth, and finally came out with her sidearm. "Take this." She shoved the butt at me. "You'll most likely fare better with two guns to shoot."

"I would," I said, "but you're doing the shooting—I'll do the running."

"I hardly think so." While she was talking, she got up to a half-crouch, like a sprinter getting ready to take off. "My boots are far better suited to running in the snow than yours, and if I'm not mistaken, my legs are somewhat longer."

"But you're a woman," I said, "and running into enemy fire… if ever something's been men's work…"

She got a look on that big face like I'd slapped her and it hurt her some. But she got it under control quick.

"It is the work of whoever happens to be best suited to it," she said soft and slow, like every word was important to her, "and it's my job; I fought to get here."

Well, I could see there was no point arguing with her, so I started to get up, figuring I could knock her down and get running before she did, or maybe keep her from even getting up in the first place.

That's when she stuck out her palm and stiff-armed me so hard I smacked down in the snow.

"Besides," she said down at me, "you'd best do the shooting; I don't believe I could shoot a man—however great the temptation."

And then she was off, sprinting through the snow like a jackrabbit.

And me, well there was nothing I could do but hunker around the corner of the Jeep and start shooting up at the cab on that tower.

I got off a round quick, just to get him looking my way, then a second one, trying to aim a little closer. I used Callie's big Army .45 'cause I figured the barrel was maybe an inch longer than my Colt .38, and with the added power of the bigger shell I might put a round up a little closer. Not that I had any hope of hitting that cab accurately, not at that range, but I figured to get his attention, like I say, whoever was up there shooting at us and maybe spoil his—

Didn't work. Not even close to working. I only got about three rounds out and up into the wild blue yonder before there was a *crack!* from the tower and Callie yelped and spun around sudden and slapped down in the snow.

Chapter 25
Six Hours After the Robbery

December 20, 1951
3:00 PM
Mort

In the room back of Lola's, Mort tried to blink the smoke out of his eyes and concentrate on his cards. *Damn,* he thought, *how long I been here?* Looked at his watch. *I gotta get out and—*

"You staying in?" Ted, the grey-haired heavyset man on his left, fingered the deck and looked at him without emotion.

Mort looked around the table. Howard had dropped out. Across from him, Boxer, the guy who never let his feelings show, seemed tense, irritated.

He don't get my luck, Mort thought, *he don't understand me being so lucky today. Hell, I don't get it myself...* He looked down at the pot. *I been riding the cards all day. Look at that: more than three hundred dollars! All the money in the world. And I can take it...*

"The man wants to know are you staying in?" Boxer's voice was different somehow. Not patient and mocking as usual, more like—Mort couldn't put his finger on it.

"Play 'em or fold 'em, dammit!" Yeah, Boxer was upset. Across the table, Howard looked at the big black man, startled.

"Hospitality's getting thin here," he tried to joke. It went nowhere.

As much good luck as I've had today, he's had bad, Mort told himself, *and I can take this pot if I want it. I can feel it already....*

He looked down at the table in front of him. He still had the fifty in his pocket, and there was a wrinkled ten still left from his betting money. He tossed the ten into the pot. "See you and raise five."

Boxer smiled. But it wasn't his usual laugh-at-whitey smile; there was something mean inside it he didn't usually let out. "See that," he tossed two bills into the pot. "And raise you fifty."

"You trying to buy the pot, Boxer?" Ted folded his cards.

"I just want to see what kind of bone ol' Lucky Mort's really got." He was keeping his voice even, but he couldn't make it sound friendly anymore. Whatever was inside him was straining at the leash now and snarling across the table at Mort.

"How 'bout it?" Ted looked over at Mort.

He's bluffing me, Mort told himself, *trying to scare me off the pot. But I can take this. I know it! All I need is…*

"Well, Mort?" Boxer wasn't smiling anymore. Wasn't even trying to pretend.

He's out for blood, Mort thought. *Well he can drink this…* He pulled the fifty from his pocket. Threw it on the table. "I call."

Boxer laid down his cards, showing two pair. "Kings and jacks." They seemed to smile up at Mort with that mocking superiority Boxer usually showed.

Everybody looks at me like that, Mort thought, *Sweeney, Magruder, even Helen sometimes. They all look at me like they know I'm never going to make anything out of myself. Like they know it, and like I'm the only one that's not in on the joke. Hell, sometimes I catch little Morty looking at me, and it's like he knows it, too; knows his Daddy's never going to amount to a hill of beans.*

He looked across the table at Boxer's smiling face, then down at the two pairs of face cards again. He laid down his cards.

Three fives, a joker and the ace of hearts.

"I think I've got this pot, gentlemen." He said it politely, like a big shot tips the doorman for hauling him a taxi. *That's me, a big shot now, with four hundred dollars and—*

"It stinks," Boxer said.

"I guess them's the breaks," Howard said it lightly, to break the obvious tension. It didn't work.

"It stinks out loud." Boxer said it slow and low, but his voice sounded different from any way they ever heard it before. Howard swallowed.

"Guess I better get back to work," he said. He got up. Slowly.

"Me, too," Ted, the grey-haired man, said, and got up carefully, keeping his hands out and one eye on Boxer. "Time to catch some air."

"I better get going myself." Mort hadn't missed a thing. He rose casually, very casually, and reached out a hand for the money on the table. "Jeez, Helen's gonna kill me for staying out all day like this. We're supposed to be at her folks' for din—"

"Get your damn hands off my money." Boxer's voice hadn't changed. "And get the hell out my place."

Mort felt dizzy. Like something had slipped away underneath him and he was falling. "Boxer," his voice sounding high and nervous in his own ears, "this is my pot. I won—"

"You cheated." Boxer was on his feet. Howard was gone and Ted was putting on his coat, his back turned deliberately, not seeing anything, not hearing. "You cheated for it. Only way a nobody like you could win off me: cheated."

"But Boxer—" Mort's voice jumped a notch higher. Like a man pleading. "Ted was dealing! You saw him! Weren't you, Ted?"

Ted still pretended not to hear. Didn't turn, made no sign. Just walked out, being extra careful not to look back.

"Now how could I cheat?" Mort caught the tone in his own voice and it made him ashamed; almost like a whimpering child.

"You had that joker tucked in your pants. I saw you sneak it out. Tried to cheat me!"

"I never—"

That was as far as he got before Boxer Healey's open left palm swung out too fast to see and connected with the right side of Mort's face.

"Calling me a liar?"

Mort didn't hear the question. His ears were ringing too loud from the force of the open-hand blow. Boxer's right hand swung out, just as fast, palm forward, and smacked against the left side of Mort's face, sending him stumbling sideways in time to catch the backswing and the cutting edge of Boxer's shiny gold ring.

Mort went to his knees, dizzy, trying to think. *Damn, I gotta... all that money...Helen...big shot...* He reached out, grasping at the bills on the table.

He never even felt the heavy beer mug come crashing down over his head.

Chapter 26
Four Hours and Twenty Minutes
After the Robbery

December 20, 1951
1:20 PM
Officer Drapp

Surprised me, how sharp it bit me, seeing a woman gunned down like that. I guess I've seen my share of nasty, in the war and since then, but that tore me up some. I felt myself go hot all over, and my eyes blurred; it was almost like I was crying, and maybe I was, and I just kept shooting up at that cab, and finally on the sixth or maybe the eighth shot, one of the windows busted out.

I didn't figure I got him, though. This just hadn't been that good a day. I put one more shot out the barrel of that .45, then dropped it in the snow and drew my Police Special and—

And then I saw she was moving.

Callie'd flipped herself over on her belly and was crawling through two foot of snow back towards the Jeep.

Not sure what got into me then. Just stupid, I guess, but for some reason I got out from behind that Jeep and run up to Callie and started pulling at the hood of her coat to help her along faster. She flapped an arm at me.

"Let go of me, you ignoramus!"

Well, folks hurt like that get crazy sometimes and I figured she didn't know what she was saying, so I kept pulling at her coat hood, and trying to keep an eye on the tower and get us back behind the Jeep, and then she cussed, like a refined college girl does—"Hug a duck!"—and got herself up on her right arm, and her left swung out and jerked my legs out from under me.

"Can't you see it hurts?" She said it like a mother bear snarls, only not sweet and patient like that. "Are you so stupid for tripe's sake?" She looked like she wanted to say more, wanted to lay me out good and proper, but then she winced and groaned. Closed her eyes and made a face ugly enough like to stop a clock and set it back an hour. Finally she could talk again and—

Crack!

The noise came from the tower, of course, but I couldn't say where it hit, or did it hit anything but snow on the ground. But I knew what I had to do.

I started running for the tower. Then, when I'd got about as far as Callie had, I stopped dead, jumped to one side and started going at right-angle across the front.

Crack!

A puff of snow flew up from right where I had been, but I wasn't anywheres close to there now. Not me. I'd stopped short and turned again and I was getting back to that Jeep like it was quitting time in Hell, and as I ran back I saw Callie had used the distraction to get back behind to safety, which is where we met up again—but not before that rifle came one more time—

Crack!

It sent a shiver up my spine like the Devil's dog had got me by the neck and shook me hard, then flung me where I landed behind the Jeep, looking at Callie's unhappy face again.

"Well, curse my bones," she said.

"Are you all right?" I asked.

"Hardly," she grunted, winced, then her eyes cleared up. "My goodness," she said. "That does hurt a bit."

"Where you hit?"

"In the left side somewhere." She tried to put an arm inside her coat to check it, but the coat was too tight-buttoned and the sleeves too thick to get it in. I reached for it myself, but she quick grabbed my wrist. "Don't touch me." She said it quiet but meaningful. "I don't want you to touch it. I'm not coughing blood so I don't believe I was hit in a lung, and I certainly wasn't hit in the heart, but there's a bullet in me and it hurts."

"Okay." I backed off, wondered what to do, then remembered what they always told us to say to a wounded man back in the war.

"You're going to be all right," I said.

"I'm most likely going to die here in the snow," she said, "unless you can think of some probable alternative."

"I will," I said, trying to figure it. "That's my job now, to get you out of here."

She got quiet a minute. Then, "I rather suspect you'll get in a bit of trouble for bringing me along with you." She talked slow and thoughtful now, like she was trying to save her energy. "Awfully sorry about that."

"Don't worry over it," I said. "I'll make up some story about how I found you out here, when we get back."

"If we get back."

"We'll get back. I'll get us out of this."

"I hardly think so," she sighed. "I have one chance to survive the day, and quite frankly I don't much fancy it."

"Whatcha mean?"

"I mean if I lie here very still, the cold will help stop my bleeding. My body will start to shiver at first, and that won't be pleasant, not with a bullet here inside me, but once that passes, and the effects of hypothermia begin to set in, my pulse and respiration will begin to slow, and that will increase my chances of survival…for a time."

"How long you figure?"

"I should say about forty minutes. If I'm not out of the cold by then...well there are long-term effects as the organs begin to shut down and brain damage occurs."

"Doesn't sound like much fun."

"I don't imagine it is. They say freezing is an easy death, but frankly I'm not anxious to try it. So if you have any good ideas—" She broke off sudden-like and gritted her teeth together as a flash of pain went through her.

Okay. It was time to figure something. And whatever I figured, I better try it quick 'cause I wouldn't get another chance. Forty minutes. I checked my watch.

Chapter 27
Four Hours and Thirty Minutes
After the Robbery

December 20, 1951
1:30 PM
Officer Drapp

That gave me till maybe 2:10. I looked over at Callie sitting there in the snow, but she was just staring off into space like she was trying to think about something besides the feel of carrying around a bullet in her. Then I twisted myself up, took a quick look up at the tower and got right back down again.

No shooting. I wondered was it maybe whoever was up there had run out of bullets, and I thought about trying to rush the tower, but again, this hadn't been such a good day that I should try my luck like that. So I looked around a little more.

A hundred yards or so of open empty behind me, the jeep in front of me, the tower beyond that, and off to my left that snow-covered car I'd been following, there at the bottom of that steep slope....

And then it come at me all at once: that wrecked car in the ditch down below was my ride out of here.

I turned to Callie sitting in the snow. "Don't go away," I said.

I jumped over to the Jeep door, flung it open, and grabbed the coiled rope from under the seat.

And then I was running, falling, sliding down the slope toward that car.

It took him by surprise—the guy in the tower, I mean. He

wasn't expecting it, and I was damn near down to the car before I heard the first shot, which didn't hit me and I don't figure it come close even, because it ain't easy to hit a moving target when you're firing down an angle like that in the blowing snow. Not that I was about to stop and check. I just slid fast as I could, and when I slowed down I got up and ran a few steps, then flung down on my belly and slid some more till I was all the way down and safe on the driver's side, with the car between me and the tower.

Whoever was up there must have got kind of upset by that, because I heard a few more shots, and one of them ping'd off the car trunk, but I paid it no mind. The driver's door of the car wasn't bent any, just half-buried, so I kicked away the snow and pulled it open.

There was a hole in the windshield, small and round and a little bigger than a bullet. And there was a man in there, facing that hole in the windshield, and his eyes they were wide open, but he wasn't seeing anything.

I stopped there a quick lifetime, just looking at the big black face with the purple knot on its forehead. His face was getting a thin coat of something shiny and grey—frost, maybe—and it looked awful big and empty.

Couldn't say, really, how it made me feel, but it wasn't good. I knew I didn't have time to squat there and look at him, but I just didn't feel like I could do anything else.

Then I saw it. A short puff of steam come from out his open mouth.

And then another.

"Hey!" I said. "You ain't dead!"

He did something that wasn't exactly moving—more like kind of a flicker behind his eyes. Like somebody had turned the lights on in his head, someplace way in the back.

"Wake up!" I said it sharp, and thought about slapping him, but that frost on his face looked like it could do him some hurt, and then I remembered something else they taught us in the army about what to do for injured folks.

"Say your name!" I shook his shoulder some. "What's your name?"

"Wha—?" Sounded like it came up to his mouth from a long ways off, but it got there.

"You got hit on the head," I said it loud and slow, "you knocked your head on the steering wheel. Now say your name. What's your name?"

"Wha—?" There was a little more sense showing now in back of his big yellow eyes, and his lips moved and his tongue come out and finally he said, "Waultah."

"Good," I said, "your name's Walter. Hang on to that. Just hold onto it—" I looked him over, felt around his body, looked over the front seat. No blood.

"Walter, you ain't even shot."

"Gummah—?" I could see he wasn't going to be much up to intellectual conversation, but he added helpfully, "Walter. Name's Walter."

"Good man," I said. "Now Walter, you just stay here a minute and try to think. Don't go to sleep or nothing, just…" I looked beyond him, at the inside of the car and over to where the passenger door was still part-open. And I just then noticed it.

Someone had left a three-gallon can of gas inside the car.

I wanted to puzzle over that. I wanted to sit there in the snow and figure long and careful about who would have brought a can of gasoline down here—from that truck sitting under the tower, most likely—and what they might have been planning to do with it. But I didn't have time for that or anything like it.

I looked in the back seat, behind Walter, and saw what I expected to see: bags and bags of money from the armored car, and a shotgun nestled comfortably among them.

I checked my watch.

Chapter 28
Four Hours and Thirty-Eight Minutes
After the Robbery

December 20, 1951
1:38 PM
Officer Drapp

So I had maybe a half-hour left to do this did I want that Callie woman not to freeze to death. Would've liked a little more margin for error so maybe I could get me a lunch break or something, but this operation wasn't run by no union rules. What I had was what I had, and I damn well better make smart use of it.

First thing, I squirmed over Walter and pulled that gas can to me and out the driver's door. Then I shrugged the coil of rope off my shoulder and started pulling big bags of money out of the back seat. The first two I laid over on Walter, one on his lap to keep him warm, the other propped on his chest to hold him upright. Then I took four more, each about the size of a big man's torso, and started running rope through the reinforced handles. Tying it off where I thought it would do the most good. I didn't stack them; I pulled them close together and overlapped the sides, jerking the knots tight as I could, because I figured this might be kind of important. I kept wanting to look at my watch, but I didn't dare slow myself up—besides Callie freezing to death, there was always a chance the guy in the tower might figure up something cute did I give him enough time for it—so I just worked fast as I could, trying to get past the cold growing in my fingers, cold making them tingle and hurt, till I had the four bags tied snug together, side to side, like kind of a blanket. Then for good measure I tied the gas can to one wrist and the shotgun up to the other, each with about a foot of slack so I could drag them through the snow.

And then I got that blanket of money bags over me and started crawling back up the slope, wondering how well this would work.

Didn't take long to find out.

Nossir, I'd likely not crawled six feet before I felt a sharp jab in my back and heard the *Crack!* of that rifle. It hurt some, but nothing like getting shot so I just kept crawling. Six feet on, there was another jab, this time near my shoulder. That hurt too, but not so much. I shrugged it off and crawled a little faster, careful not to stick my arms or legs too far out from under my money-bag blanket. Another shot, this one like a punch in the kidney, and I heard myself groan, but I kept moving.

Kept moving through the snow, which was about up to my face when I crawled. Kept feeling the cold of it through my heavy gloves and the knees of my pants. Cold like a sharp-stabbing hurt. And for some damn reason I kept hearing that godawful, slogging Christmas song, the one that was playing when I first walked into that ranger station, right before everything went to hell on a fast horse. Like marching music in my head:

> *Westward leading,*
> *Still proceeding,*
> *Guide us to,*
> *Thy perfect light….*

Guide us someplace anyhow. I raised my head to see where the hell I was going and got a quick splash of snow right in front of my face and heard the sharp *Crack!* of that damn rifle when the guy in the tower took another try at me.

I was getting close to the top of the slope now. And the road. And the Jeep. I could taste salt in my mouth from the snot running out my nose, my hands ached from the chill and my knees even worse. Like I got bit or something every time I put them down in all that misery. Hurt so bad I hated to keep on doing it, but I had to, and I hated it that I had to. The strain of dragging that gas can and shotgun through two feet of snow didn't help none either, but there wasn't nothing I could do but just keep at it, keep crawling up through that white grief.

Star of won-der,
Star of light,
Star of roy-al,
Beauty bright….

And I got to say, the guy in the tower didn't like it much.

I heard a volley of *CRACK-CRACK-CRACK!* from up his way, but he must have been getting rattled because I didn't feel none of them. All I felt was the nasty burning sting of ice-cold air hitting my face, and the hurt in my hands and knees, which had turned to tingling now, almost numb, and I got to wondering would a bullet feel better than this cold, and then next I knew I was back behind the Jeep with Callie.

She looked at me, covered with money bags.

"You." She gritted the word out through clenched teeth and I saw how she was concentrating, doing everything she could not to shiver. "Quite clever."

"Stuff they make these bags out of," I said, hugging close to the car and putting my gloved hands on the tailpipe, feeling the welcome touch of it like the sun on a warm day or a kiss from a pretty woman. "Can't cut it, can't even shoot through it. And the money inside takes the shock of the bullet—mostly, anyway."

"Wonderful."

It seemed like all at once, she quit shivering, quit concentrating, and I figured that likely wasn't a good sign. "How you holding up?" I asked.

She thought some about that. "This isn't nearly as pleasant as I'd been led to believe," she said finally. "Do you suppose you could hurry things up a bit?"

"Just as much as I can. But we got another problem; there's a man down there in that car, mostly froze to death, and I don't think he's your Captain Scranton. "

"A policeman?"

"I don't figure he's a policeman, no."

"Is he shot?"

"Naah." I shrugged under the money-bag blanket and snuck a look up at the tower. "Whoever shot at him shot from that tower; they missed, but the car went down that embankment and hit something that stopped it sudden-like. This guy inside he banged his head, knocked him out."

"He's not a policeman?"

"He doesn't look like one." I figured it was the cold making her mind lose track of what I told her. "Anyway, I brought him around but I sure couldn't do much about warming him up."

"He must be…." She started, then trailed off, like talking was hard, or maybe she just couldn't keep her mind on it. Then she just started up again, "He'll have been warmer in that car, but still… We must help him."

"Crossed my mind, too."

"You're going to the tower now?"

"Can't walk around it."

"The tower is a hundred and nine feet tall at the tip," she said in kind of a sing-song voice, like a schoolgirl reciting a lesson. "There are nine levels, not including the cab, which is six feet square. There are twelve steps each for the first two levels, which are four feet wide…"

I looked at her hard, but she just kept going in that say-your-lessons voice.

"…eight steps apiece for the last seven levels, which start at three feet wide, but narrow to two feet, then to eighteen inches…"

I figured this must be the spiel she gave to tourists, and kind of wondered where she thought she was. Made a chill run through me worse than the cold to hear her go on like that. I put my hands around the warm tailpipe again and wished I could put my knees there too.

"…similarly, the platforms at the landings are four feet wide to begin with, but will narrow to eighteen inches toward the top. The tower was built in 1936 as part of the public works project initiated by President Franklin D. Roosevelt…"

I didn't stick around to hear the rest.

Chapter 29
Four Hours and Fifty Minutes
After the Robbery

December 20, 1951
1:50 PM
Officer Drapp

Twenty minutes left to get this done. I needed a cigarette, needed it painful hard, but I figured Callie'd likely take it the wrong way was I to stop for a smoke. So instead I just put my face some ways closer to that warm tailpipe on the Jeep, trying not to breathe the fumes of it, and warmed up as much as I could for a few seconds. Then I tried not to think too much about anything as I shrugged the money-bag blanket back over me and started crawling to the tower.

I gotta give this to the guy up there in the cab: he was wising up. I heard three shots all that time I took crawling, but I only felt one of them, like a sharp jab on the back of my butt. Another one hit close to the gas can and shotgun I was dragging at the end of the ropes tied to my wrists, but I didn't even see the next, so I figured he was shooting for my legs and feet when they stuck out behind me. Smart feller. I made my crawl-steps smaller and the shooting stopped.

There was a snow fence partway around the base of that tower made up from six-foot wooden slats held together with chicken wire, with an opening to park the truck. When I reached it I figured I was too close to the tower for him to shoot down at me, so I stood up—Lord, it felt good to get my knees out of that cold, wet, icy death!—and I saw the snow was drifted up against that fence almost as high as my shoulders. I squeezed past the service truck and then I was under the tower itself. Looked at my watch and saw I'd done the forty yards in three minutes, which wasn't burning up any speed records, but I was pretty happy with it. I checked the steps overhead to make sure was there nobody coming down them and

　Crack!

Damn, but I was getting sick of that noise. I heard a quick *ping-ping!* as the shot ricocheted off the steps above me. I pulled the money bags mostly over my head and peeked out from under.

Near as I could see there was a trapdoor under the cab up there and he was sticking the rifle out it trying to shoot me, which would have been a tricky proposition even in good times. In the middle of a blizzard like this, it was a dope-dream. So I tried not to worry too much about it while I dug the jackknife out of my pants pocket and cut loose one of the money bags to use as a shield.

I say I tried not to worry about it, but the *Crack-ping-ping!* of him shooting at me got on my nerves some while I figured on what I wanted to carry up the steps with me: I wanted the shotgun and the gas can and my Colt .38 in my hand or where I could get it. I'd need to grab the handrail going up those ice-covered steps and hang onto it hard, and I wanted to hold the money bag in front of me, so I'd got to have at least three hands did I want to do this thing right. And then there was the problem with my gloves. I'd sure need them to hang onto that metal stair-rail, but the problem with gloves was that any glove good enough to keep my hands warm was also too thick to get my finger inside the trigger guard of that Colt. So if I had to keep my hands warm and carry the money bag for a shield and still shoot anybody very much…

I suddenly realized I was standing around there in the snow, just thinking. Thinking too much, too long. And too slow. Checked my watch again, and near as I could see I'd just used up another five minutes.

Well damn and double-damn. I reached under my coat, got the .38 out of my flap holster and stuffed it up my right-hand sleeve. Hell of a lot easier to shake it down out of my sleeve than try to dig under my coat and get into my holster for it. Then I cut me some rope and used it to loop the gas can over one shoulder. Cut more rope and looped the shotgun over the other shoulder. That left me a hand to hold the money bag and a hand to grab onto whatever there was to grab onto while I went up the steps.

Crack-ping-ping-piinnggg!

Time to start climbing.

Three steps up my feet went out from under me on the icy step and I fell flat on my face. I pulled myself up under the weight of the gas can and the shotgun and the money bag and took the steps slower, trying to keep my body centered over my feet while I climbed, trying to look where I was stepping and look out for something coming down from above all at the same time.

I made the first landing, nice, wide and open, and I almost slipped clean off it getting to the next flight of steps.

Funny what I thought of then: When I was a kid I used to dream I could fly, and in my dreams it really felt like I was sailing around the skies, with nothing under my kicking legs, nothing to hold onto, and everything spinning around me as I just scudded off every which way there was. That came back to me then; that's almost how it felt climbing those steps, with the snow blowing around me like a crazy-spinning tide, and my feet sliding all over, and everything I tried to hang onto covered with slippery ice.

Look up. Look down. Hold the money bag up. Climb. Slip. Get up and climb again. Underneath me it was like those steps would shift and twist and jerk sidewise on their own, but I knew it was just the wind and the ice. Had to be. They couldn't really be rolling under my feet like I was walking through a fun-house—could they? I felt myself getting dizzy and closed my eyes to shut out the snow swirling around me like sudsy water running down a drain.

Sudsy water. Down the drain.

I could almost see the bubbles, white and round and sparkle-shiny as they swirled around and down and around and down and around and down.

Damn.

I made myself open my eyes again. Just in time for

CRACK-ping-PING!

I swear I felt metal fly past my ear, and one thing I'll say: it woke me up some, it did. I set down the bag, pushed the handgun out my sleeve, aimed between the steps, and squeezing best I could with my gloves still on, put a shot up overhead. Didn't hit anything. Didn't look to, but it sure shut up that noisy neighbor upstairs.

I jammed the handgun back up my sleeve. Time to get going again. How high up was I? I'd lost track of steps, landings and what-else, and when I looked down it made me too dizzy to count.

So nothing for it but to climb up some more steps. Like there was nothing in the world anymore but steps to climb. Hold on tight, try not to think about it when my foot slipped close to the open side of the stairs and my weight started to shift out into thin air—I pulled back and kept climbing.

Two more flights up I made the mistake of looking down. The sight of all that snowy open underneath got me sick to my stomach. I felt the dry-heaves start, and I fought them back. *No time to get sick right now; save it for later, and vomit when you can sit back and enjoy it.*

The steps were getting narrower, the landings smaller, the turns tighter as I squeezed around them, holding that money-bag up where I figured it to do me some good. The guy upstairs took another shot but I didn't hear it even hit nothing, so he was likely getting bothered-up some. I sure hoped so. I looked overhead and saw I only had maybe two more flights to go, and just then the trapdoor slammed shut, so I guess he decided to quit shooting and just fort up in the cab there.

Which made the next part of my job easier. I got up those last two flights quick as I could—which wasn't real quick at all—set the gas can on the step under the trapdoor and unslung the shotgun from behind me. Took off the glove from my shooting hand. Then one last time I checked my watch.

Chapter 30
Five Hours and Twelve Minutes
After the Robbery

I was too late.

It hit my cold-numbed brain like a snowball in my face. I'd used up all my time and more getting up this damn stairway to hell, and even could I shoot this bastard now and get on with it, well, it'd be too late; by the time I got back down to her, that ranger-lady, she'd be froze to death or close enough to make no difference.

I felt myself going into that mad-crazy feeling, like I had when I'd seen her get shot: all wrenched up inside me, and maybe I was screwy from the cold, but I swear I could feel my fingers around the neck of that guy I'd never even seen, the man on the other side of the floor over my head.

I turned it off.

Just turned it off. Made myself stop and breathe and get rid of all that hot hate. Was I going to do this—and that was a long ways from a sure thing—I better stay cool at it. Keep my feelings out of this, sell him on the notion of coming out where I could shoot him easy, then kill him fast and efficient. And maybe dance on his grave some.

I looked at the gas can set there on the top step and called out, "Howdy up there."

No answer.

"I'm Officer Drapp, Willisburg Police. We ain't been introduced, but I'd guess you to be Captain Scranton."

No answer.

I went on, "Well Captain, I'd sure like for you to open that trapdoor—just so you do it slow, real slow—and toss out that rifle and your sidearm. Then ease yourself down out of there with your hands out where I can see 'em."

Still no answer. Maybe it was time for some of that sharp police-method questioning.

"So whatcha doing for Christmas this year?" I asked. "You got any big plans or just a bunch of parties?"

That finally got me an answer.

"Why'nch y'all come up and get me, copper!"

Come up and get me, copper?

"You need to get out to the movies more," I said. "Nobody talks like that these days."

"Ah said come on up in hyah." The voice had that smooth, Deep South honey-sweet ring to it, that way of talk that sounds real down-homey and inviting sometimes. But right now it was hard, raspy, and just a little bit the other side of plain crazy. "Or mebbe you ain't got the guts, yah yeller sumbitch!"

I guess he was trying to get me mad again, maybe as mad as he was. Well, I knew better than that.

"I ain't got the stupids is what I ain't got," I said. "No call for me to go up there when we're both of us coming back down, now is there?"

"Well, I sure's hell ain't coming out, you yellow chickenshit cop!"

"Suit yourself," I said, "but I got me a gas can—the one you took down to burn out that car down there till you saw it was full of money. I got that gas can and I set it right under here and real quick now I'm going to get tired of this and build me a fire under your butt. And then I'm going to just head back down and let you burn—like how you was going to do the guy in that car."

No answer.

"I ain't counting to three or nothing." I pointed the shotgun at the trapdoor. "Just you get used to the notion this ain't your party now; it's my party and I'm going to get tired of waiting real sudden and set fire to you. You don't want that, you'd best do like I said."

No answer.

I fished under my coat to get the lighter out of my pocket. Then,

"Okay y'all stinking yellow copper. I'm coming out."

"You come out too fast I'll take your face off with this shotgun." I figured he'd seen me tote it up the slope here. "So better you just open that door slow and drop out your rifle and sidearm."

The door opened. Slow. The barrel of his hunting rifle dropped into view. *Should have told him butt-first,* I thought, *but—*

I cradled the shotgun in one arm, reached up quick left-handed and jerked down on the barrel of that rifle, hard and fast. It held back for a second, then came loose and clattered down the steps and off the tower.

"Y'all happy now, copper?" The voice from over my head, harsh and shrill and stupid. "I'm coming out!"

"Toss out your sidearm first."

"I ain't got any," he said. "I say I'm unarmed, you stinking chicken copper. You going to shoot me unarmed?"

Well, I was going to shoot him sure enough, I knew that much anyhow. This wasn't the kind of situation where I could take any prisoners, even did I feel like it, which I didn't much.

And maybe he didn't have a handgun and maybe Santa Claus was coming to town, but I wasn't making bets on either one of them. I snugged my finger closer around the trigger of that shotgun and waited.

A big ugly hiking boot showed through the trapdoor, coming out slow. Then another. I set back the gas can to give him room and to get back out of the way for when he tried to kick me. His green-khaki legs came out, and then the bottom of his coat, and finally he was almost all the way out. I got a quick look at a big square body, like you see on somebody if he's grown up playing football or something, and his face—I only saw it just real quick, but it had that bloated-up dead-and-wrinkled kind of look like a man that's handled more booze than Jack Daniels. His hands were still up out of sight, maybe holding onto something up there so he wouldn't slip, maybe raised in surrender—but most likely holding a handgun.

And this was no place for momma's little boy to go taking chances; time to blow his belly out his backside. I braced myself against the step, tucked the shotgun in close and squeezed the trigger.

It didn't work.

The shotgun had froze up on me and I was holding three feet of useless steel.

And looking up the muzzle of his Army .45.

I tossed the shotgun up at him just as he fired. It bounced off the step underneath him and bounced back and hit me in the face and I hardly even felt it, I was scrambling back so fast. I heard the sharp, nasty *snap!* of his .45 going off not six feet away, but I didn't feel anything except the dull thud of that cold shotgun across my frozen face, so maybe he missed me. I didn't know. Didn't have time to think at it. I was just moving fast as I could, jumping backward, slipping, falling down the stairs.

I backstepped-slid-fell down eight steps to the landing, twisted my body around so I wouldn't slide off the edge, angled to the flight underneath, twisted-slid-fell down that flight and likewise the one below that. Two shots hit something overhead, but I had no way of knowing did they get close to me. Somewhere in the back of my mind I figured if I could get enough steps between us I might have a split-second to jerk the .38 out of my right sleeve and maybe another split second to take a shot back up at him. Those didn't seem like good odds, but they were the best I was going to get today, and with my head hitting those steps *thud-thud-thud* I didn't have time to think of anything better. So I twist-slid down the next set of steps, grabbed a rail to turn my body, and—

And it was covered with ice.

I felt myself slide out to the edge of the landing about the same time my fingers slipped off the rail. And then I was just flying loose. Nothing underneath me but cold cold air and I was spinning through empty space, just like when I was a kid, dreaming I could fly.

Chapter 31
Five Hours and Twenty Minutes
After the Robbery

December 20, 1951
2:20 PM
Officer Drapp

Next thing I knew, I was dead.

It sure felt dead, anyway. Everything around me was cold and white and I wasn't breathing and there wasn't any air in my lungs. Seemed like I'd stopped falling, though. I couldn't move my arms or legs, but I rolled my eyes and saw nothing but white all around.

Yeah, I must be dead.

Sure was cold here.

But for some reason my lungs were screaming for air. And when I tried to breathe, it was like somebody had a foot on my chest, pressing down. I bucked up and down best I could, and opened my mouth and managed to inflate my lungs again. The air was so cold it hurt, but I made myself take three or four more deep breaths.

So I figured I wasn't dead. It made sense; where I was headed in the next world, it sure wasn't going to be cold.

I tried moving my arms and legs again and now I could feel they were surrounded by snow. I was on my back looking up, and I couldn't roll over, but I could bend my knees and elbows some. I started punching and kicking, and after a time of that I had a little room to wiggle around and then a little more room and finally I could twist over on my hands and knees and start crawling out of the five-foot-deep snow drift I'd fallen into.

I reasoned out that I'd slipped maybe halfway down those steps before I fell off the tower and then dropped maybe forty-fifty feet and landed in that shoulder-high drift next to the snow fence. That's as near as I could figure how come I to be still alive, anyhow. Did all this figuring while I was kicking and crawling my way out to where the snow was only a foot or so high, and about the time I got clear, I started wondering whatever happened to the guy up in the tower.

And just about then his boot connected with my face.

That answered that question.

Now me, I was brought up not to kick a man when he's down, but that's just me. This guy, I guess his old man never taught him that. It must have struck him funny even, because he laughed when he did it.

Cold as I was, that laugh sent a whole 'nother shiver right up my back; the deep-down crazy sound of a man about to do something awful and do it up right and have fun while he's at it—a whole lot of fun.

I tried to shake off the ringing in my ears and do something about the cold fear I was feeling, and just then I got another kick, this one deep in my left side.

I was so padded up with my police jacket and heavy over-coat, I barely felt it. But I rolled with it, over on my back into the deep snow and yelled like he'd broke a rib or something.

"Whose party now, copper?"

He come clomping through the snow at me. I looked up at him, and was there any doubt in my mind I was dealing with a man gone mean-crazy, I lost it right then. That look of pure simple pleasure in his face told me everything about the situation, and it wasn't good news, not at all.

I saw him pull back his leg for another one, and I tried to roll with that one too, but I couldn't do much about it on my back in the snow. I managed to get over back onto my hands and knees, though, and slam my right fist down into the packed snow underneath me.

Another kick. I tried to put some distance between us—but not too much; I figured he still had that .45 and I didn't want him to use it any more than he had already. No, I figured to just keep him happy with kicking me around for a while.

"Don't you want to know," I said, though it was hard talking through cold air and a kicked-in body, "about the money?"

I guess not. He stepped over, his boots crashing down through the snow, and gave me another kick.

"Don't *you* want to know," he asked all breathless and shrill, "how slow you're going to die?"

Well, nossir, I didn't care to learn much about that at all. But nothing I could do about it, lying on my back there in the snow. He reached down somewhere I couldn't see and came up holding the three-gallon gas can. And I mean he was holding it up to make sure I saw it real good.

"Going to burn me out with this, were you?" He wasn't asking like he wanted an answer. While I kept moving around like a squashed bug, trying to get back over on my hands and knees, he hefted the gas can, unscrewed the cap and went on talking.

"...come all the way out here in your cop car full of money trying to frame me up for stealing it and that bitch with you for a witness. All the time just setting me up with that damn shoe-shine boy driving your stinking cop car?"

It come to me then just how crazy he was; here he'd come across a car full of money—I mean from up there he just saw it was a police car coming, and maybe figured someone was coming to get him or like that, but then he took his shot at it and went down and saw it was full of money bags—and still the thought going through his head when he saw all that dough was that it meant everyone was out to get him.

He got a good grip on the can, getting ready to dump it out on me and then he laughed again, like it struck him funny all over. "Did that boy know I was going to shoot him dead?"

We both heard the voice behind him at the same time.

"You missed him, you know." It was weak and out of breath and strained with hurting, but it still sounded all high class and refined, like that movie actress that I can't think of her name.

She went on, "I'm afraid you're simply not that good a shot, Captain."

Chapter 32
Five Hours and Thirty-Two Minutes
After the Robbery

December 20, 1951
2:32 PM
Officer Drapp

That Scranton guy, he turned and looked. Me, I rolled over and got up on my hands and knees. Callie was standing in the snow, not twenty feet away from us. Or maybe I don't mean to say she was standing; the way she was on her feet she looked like a boatload of sailors trying to dance the ballet in a hurricane. She had one hand pressed up at her side, like to ease the pain or stop the bleeding, and the other was swinging around for balance and when she stopped moving it looked like the only thing holding her up was the snow up to her knees.

I pounded my right fist into the snow again while she said in a voice like she was serving tea, "And as you don't seem much good with it, perhaps you'd best simply throw down your gun and let the officer arrest you."

Well the plan had my vote, but I guess he didn't much want to do that. Scranton just got a meaner look on his big, beefy face and I pounded my right fist in the snow again and he said, all quiet and sincere, "You're going to wish you were dead a long time before I finish with you." The quietness made him sound even crazier, if you know what I mean.

He hugged the gas can in one arm, set his legs in a shooter's stance and leveled his gun at her like he wanted to do this up right; maybe shoot her in someplace real special.

Only he never got to because I pounded my fist into the snow one more time and that finally shook the gun loose that I'd shoved up my sleeve. It slid down into my hand and I swung up and snapped off a shot.

Scranton's right leg jerked up sudden and got a big red spot on it, right at the knee, then kicked up in front of him like he was back on his college football field. His left leg slipped out from under him and his gun arm swung wide and fired off at no place special, and then he was on his back in the snow and the gas can spilling all over him.

Good shot.

I got up off my knees and steadied myself just in time to see him sit up and look around for me. We both brought our guns up about the same time, and I was just enough ahead of him to make it count.

Or maybe not. He got off one round and I got off two, aiming for the center of mass, like they showed me in the Army, but I was shooting like a deacon in a whorehouse; one shot went into his right shoulder and the other clear missed him. Meantime, I saw his .45 spit at me and I heard something whistle past my ear with a sound like to turn my insides to water.

But that was the last shot he ever fired because right after he shot my one good round went into his shoulder there. His gun arm went all rubbery, the .45 flew out of his hand and buried itself in snow, and he hit the ground on his back again, nice and hard.

I just stood there on my knees a few seconds, watching to see did he try to get back up, but he didn't look to be doing it any time soon, so I turned to look at Callie.

Couldn't find her.

Just didn't see her anywhere around. I got up on my feet and then I could see she'd fallen and the snow was so deep all around I couldn't see her till I was standing up.

She was lying in the snow. Real still.

I got over to her and first thing I saw was the fog from her breathing, so I figured she was all right, or at least not much worse hurt than when I left her.

I was wrong.

Soon as I got close I could see a dark spot on her coat where that wound must have bled clear through the heavy fabric, and her face was nearly as white as the snow around her. Must have cost her a lot of pain and blood to get over here through all that. I wondered how she could have done it when by rights she should have been froze to death or pretty close to it. But all I could figure to say was, "You all right?"

"I've been better." She opened her eyes. "Did you get him?"

"Got him good enough to make a difference." I opened her coat and she was past shivering in the cold. So far past she never even noticed it.

It looked ugly.

Her left side, down under the chest, it was red and wet and still bleeding. Not pumping blood, which was a good sign not to see, but bleeding plenty fast enough.

"That was a damn fool thing you did, coming over here," I said.

"It's my job," she said simply. "You said there was a civilian. Down in that car," She stopped and took a breath. "It's my job to protect visitors to this park."

"Well, it ain't your job to bleed to death." I unbuckled the belt from her pants and slipped it out, then undid the heavy scarf from around her neck. "How the hell'd you keep from freezing to death out there?"

"It's simply my job," she said again, like it was important to her, and I guess it was. "When I heard him shooting at you, I reasoned he might be preoccupied, so I got under the Jeep." She stopped to breathe again. "Not an easy trip. But warmer there," she managed.

"Well it was still a damnfool thing to do, pardon my French." I folded the scarf and put it against the wound, then looped her belt around it and pulled it tight. She made a little sound when I fastened the buckle to hold it. Not a pretty sound, either. "I mean yeah, you likely saved my life, coming up when you did, and—" My nose was running, from the cold or something, and I blew it on my coat sleeve. "I guess I'm glad you did it but you had no call to go killing yourself that way over the likes of me."

"I'm not dead," she said, "and I won't be if you go about this properly."

"Think I got the bleeding stopped," I said. "Now I got to get you over to the truck there. It might hurt some."

"I can move myself."

"You try getting up and I'll knock you flat again and if you don't think I can do it, you just start." I tried to sound mean enough to stop her just by talking. "You go dying now, and who's gonna clean up all the mess around here? Now lie down and let me do this proper."

I put her arms down at her sides, zipped her coat up, then grabbed her by the hood and started dragging her through the snow. And I'm here to tell you it wasn't no picnic. Nossir. That woman was a lot of beef to be moving around. I had to grab onto her hood like a bible at a tent meeting, and lean way over, use all my weight to get her moving through the snow.

Got it done, though.

I hauled her to the truck under the tower there. It was closer than the Jeep and no one had put a bullet through the windshield, so I figured to use it getting out of here. And besides, I was going to need a truck for what had to be done. On the way there, I looked over at Scranton; I didn't figure him to have bled to death yet, but he wasn't moving any either.

Fine.

We reached the truck and I got in and it started up easy, which was a relief. I cranked the heat up as far as I could and put the blower on High. There was an olive-drab metal lunch box on the seat and I threw it in the back before I got out again and bent down to Callie there in the snow. "How you doing now?"

"A bit dizzy, I'm afraid." She sounded tired, too. "Can you help me into the truck?"

"I can help you some," I said. "Let's get to it."

Damn, that woman was heavy. Not soft-and-fat heavy, but solid heavy, like a big tree or a live cow or something. She helped some once we got her legs under her, and I got her in the truck okay, but I was winded and sweaty by the time it was done, and she kept making these little sounds, like she was trying not to scream with the pain of doing it.

"Much nicer." She laid down across the truck seat and sounded kind of dreamy-like. I pushed her farther in, so her head was raised up a little on the driver-side door. "Thank you so much."

"Very welcome." I could feel warm air starting to blow from the heater in there, and I wanted to climb in and sit down beside her and rest my weary bones while I told her the sad story of my life. But there was work to do. I decided to split the difference and lit a cigarette and took a deep draw on it, feeling it kick my heart some and give me that false sense of well-being you get from having a smoke at the right time.

Then a thought hit me—and I mean to say it crossed my mind like a runaway train: I'd just lit a cigarette. And I was standing outside.

I looked around me. Sometime in the middle of all this, when I didn't think to sit up and take notice, the snow had stopped and the wind quit.

That meant my time was going to start running out, and damn quick, too.

"You lie down here," I said. "Keep yourself still. I got some things here need finishing up."

I'll give her this: she laid down like I told her to. But she said, "The man down in the car. Can you get him up here by yourself?"

"Hadn't thought about it," I said. "Guess I'll have to, anyhow."

"Use the—" she started, then winced with pain a couple seconds before she could get on with it, "—the Jeep. Get rope from the truck if you need more. Then use the Jeep. "

"Thanks," I said, wondering what the hell she was talking about, 'use the Jeep.' "You just lie here a spell, and try not to bleed any more than you can help it."

I took the rope from the back of the truck and it was stiff from cold but useable. And there'd be more in the Jeep, which is where I headed.

On the way back over there I looked in on Captain Scranton again. He was coming right along, lying there in the snow, reeking from the spilled gas all over him. His left hand was pressed up to his shoulder where I'd shot it, and he had his mostly limp right arm down at his leg, pressing hard as he could up to the hole I'd put in it. I guess he'd stopped the bleeding some but we both knew he couldn't keep it up long.

"Git some bandages on me, you dayyam yankee." Again with the corn-pone talk. Maybe I couldn't blame him was that the best he could do, come a time like this. "You gotta stop this bleeding 'fore you take me in, damya!"

I stood there and looked down at him a minute.

"Y'all gonna let me freeze to death?" He snarled it out like he was giving me orders. Maybe he was.

"They say that's an easy death," I said.

Then I took a last drag off my cigarette and tossed it down onto his gas-soaked coat.

Chapter 33
Five Hours and Forty-Seven Minutes
After the Robbery

December 20, 1951
2:47 PM
Officer Drapp

Back at the Jeep I tried to figure what that crazy ranger-lady meant when she said *use the Jeep*. Didn't make sense, from what I could see. A few years later they put winches on a Jeep which you could mount on the front and haul stuff up to it—or more likely hook to a tree and pull yourself out when the tires won't do it. But that wasn't invented yet back when I'm telling this, so I guessed she was just talking fever-talk. I looked in the back anyway, though, to see was there a clue in there maybe about what she said.

Nothing there but more of that rope I used before to tie the money bags together. Lots of it, coiled up nice and neat like they teach you in the Boy Scouts. So much I wondered did she put it there for something and just now thought to tell me about it. Must have been near a half-mile just of rope.

I got it.

I picked up as much as I could and hoisted it over my shoulder. Then I grabbed some more and headed back down the slope to the wrecked car, mostly by sliding and falling.

The guy inside was still kind of just staring off into space, but he looked a little sharper. I barked his name.

"Walter! Hey Walter! Over here!"

Slowly—and I mean real slow—he looked over at me with blank stupid eyes.

"Whuh?"

So he still wasn't much for conversation.

"Walter, wake up," I said. "I gotta get you out of here, Walter, and it's going to hurt."

"It hurts," he said like that idea come to him for the first time right this minute. "Cold. Hurts."

"Yeah I know," I said, "that's why we gotta get you out of here. Can you move your legs okay?"

I waited a half-minute while he got his mind around the notion of moving his legs, and then he actually started moving them. Maybe like frozen molasses, but he was moving. Good sign.

"Good job, Walter." I got him out and away from the car and laid him down in the snow.

Callie was right. He was too heavy for me to get up that slope and he sure wasn't going up there on his own.

"Walter," I said, "this is going to hurt some more. Can you take it?"

That bucked him up a little. He looked at me kind of like it was a challenge, but all he said was, "What's that noise?"

"It's the wind." I looped the rope under his arms and tied it off good and solid in a bow line knot: the kind that makes a loop that won't tighten, and I still had plenty more to play with.

"Sounds…" He squinted, like maybe he thought squinting would make him hear it better. "Sounds like somebody screaming."

"Yeah," I said, "it does, kind of."

I hand-hauled the rest of the money bags out of the car, dragging them out lined up in the snow. Then I threaded the rope through the handles—like I was stacking keys on a chain, with Walter there at the bottom. I looked over at him, lying in the snow with a rope around his chest.

"How you doing there?"

"Burns." He said it high-pitched from the hurt of it. "It burns. Why they burn me?"

"Hell, that's a good sign." I hoped so, anyway. "It's the cold burning. Means you're gonna be all right."

"I don't want 'em to burn me." He sighed it, kind of dreaming or something.

Well, I had work to do.

It was a long trek back up the slope, playing out the rope behind me, but I made it up to the tower and under one of the round metal legs, then over to the Jeep where I tied the end of the rope to the tow hook in back. Tied it solid.

And then I got in the Jeep and angled it just right, down what was left of the tracks that car had made going down the slope, set it in low, let out the clutch, and jumped out just as I felt it start to move down the slope.

Worked like a wonder dog. The Jeep went down, tugging the rope out as it went, Walter and the money bags came up, pulled by the weight of the Jeep, and I was there to cut everything loose when they got where I wanted them.

Then I looked down and saw the Jeep hit the back of that car down there and push it past whatever it was hung up on at the edge of the lake. I watched as the car cruised out onto the ice, slipping sidewise, and then I saw the snow over the lake start to shake and shift and then the car just disappeared under the ice.

About time something came my way easy today.

Walter got into the truck mostly on his own but I had to lift Callie's legs up since she was still lying across the whole bench seat and set him under her bent knees. I couldn't see that she'd bled any onto the seat, and I figured that was likely a good thing.

I made introductions. "This is Park Ranger Callie Nixon. Callie, this is the guy from the car down there. The one you told me how to get him up here."

She cleared her throat, winced some from the hurt of it, and said, "Welcome to Boothe National Park."

"Ummah-gummah," he replied.

She looked up at me. "You said he was in the car down there."

"That's right."

"But that looked like a police car."

"And I'm a policeman," I said. "See how it works?"

"But he's not a policeman."

"That's right."

"He was in the car, though."

"I've got things to do," I said, "I'll be back in a minute and tell you all about it." I was just about to get away when she grabbed my sleeve.

"What was that awful noise?" she asked.

"It was the wind."

"It's stopped now."

"That's right." I looked over at the traces of smoke and steam still rising from the black smudge in the snow where Captain Scranton used to be. "It's stopped now."

Chapter 34
Six Hours and Fifteen Minutes
After the Robbery

It took some doing, but I finally got us rolling. We were in the truck with Callie's head on my right leg and her knees bent across Walter's lap and eleven bags of money loaded in the back of the truck.

Nice work, but it wasn't going to be real easy pushing through snow all the way to Bootheville General Hospital, which was where we needed to go did I want to keep that woman on my leg alive.

That woman on my leg. She moved a little and looked up past my elbows at me.

"I'm not sure how long I can stay awake, and I need to tell you this." Her voice was still refined and classy, but it sounded far-off.

"Better just rest," I said. "Tell me later."

"I'm not completely sure I may be here later. And I'm quite certain you won't be."

"Don't talk dumb," I said. "You're going to be fine and we'll have plenty of time to talk it all over once I get you to the hospital."

"No, I'm not dying; dying is a sign of weakness, and I'm not about to permit it, but when I wake up I rather think you'll be gone."

"How come?"

"Because you're the bank robber, you know…."

"Sounds like you got your brains froze out there," I said, "I'm Officer Drapp, Willisburg Police."

"No," she said, "you're the bank robber."

"There wasn't any bank robber," I said. "Those guys I was after, they hit an armored car. So they'd be armored-car robbers."

"You said that back at the Office and I told you then it was neither here nor there, and it's in rather the same place now." She stopped to take a breath. "Bank, car or Cracker Jack box, I believe you're the robber."

"I still say your brains is froze." I slowed for a curve, easing up on the pedal and working the clutch, which wasn't real easy with her big ugly head on my leg. "But how you figure?"

"It seemed a bit odd, back at the office when you arrived in a farm truck, you'll admit that."

"Yeah, I told you it was better for—"

"Better for driving in the snow, you said that." Even on a half-tank of blood she ran right over what I was saying. "And then you didn't call for other police officers when you should have."

"I thought I told you about Chief Peanut back there."

"Yes, and I listened politely but I didn't actually believe you, you know." She stopped real quick, like she wanted to make a noise or something to do with the hurt she was in. But then she just bit it back and kept talking. "And then when we found the car, it looked a bit like a police car and you didn't seem at all surprised."

"Couldn't really see it that good."

"Nor were you surprised at this man who is not a policeman

being in the car. And you knew it was full of money. You got the idea of going down there and using those money bags as a shield —because you knew they'd be there."

"Like I told you. I was following the getaway car."

"Which looked a bit like a police car and here you are…" She stopped a second, like the talk was wearing her out. I sure hoped so. "…dressed as a policeman," she finally finished it.

"I told you how all that happened," I said, "and I'm dressed like a cop because I happen to be one: Officer Drapp, Willisburg Police."

"I rather doubt it. But you confirmed my theory when you stood up."

"Hunh?"

She had to take another breath before she went on. "When we were first fired upon and we took cover behind the car. When we weren't certain who it might be up in the tower. Then you stood up and waved and let him see you. Because you thought it might be your partner up there."

"Yeah, but he near killed me for it." I worked on my driving and balanced her head on my leg. "Or did you forget that?"

"That's when you knew it was my captain up there," she said, "and that's when I became certain that you were the robber. Or rather, you were one of the robbers. Is this other gentleman your partner?"

"When he comes to, I'll ask him." I chewed my lip and tried to think at what she said and move a truck full of sick, injured, and money all at the same time, and finally I came back with, "But I guess it's like you said; it ain't neither here or there."

"I beg your pardon?"

"Listen," I said, "I'm Officer Drapp. Like I told you. But even was I wasn't, what's the difference?"

"The difference is rather obvious, don't you think?"

"The difference is I'm the guy who pulled you out of the

snow and took care of that bastard—excuse me—that Scranton guy that shot you open and then I got you in the truck here and I'm taking you to the hospital. Be I a cop or be I a robber, that's me and this is what I'm doing. You maybe saved my life back there and now I'm saving yours, and I don't figure you're going to arrest me or nothing, so what does it make for shucks am I a cop or a robber?"

That stopped her a minute and I went on, "But I happen to be Officer Drapp and I wish you'd remember it, does anyone ask."

"Cops and robbers," she said it all dreamy-like, then she kind of looked up past me and her voice got funny and she said, "I'm going away now."

Her eyes glazed up and the lids fluttered. Her whole body seemed to go limp as running water all at once, and she made kind of a funny sound. I'd heard it once before, and I hadn't heard any sound like it since the war, one time when a non-com got shot and fell over and died right over top of me: it was the death rattle. The sound of air bubbling out the lungs one last time. The sound a body makes when the soul goes away wherever it's going and leaves just an empty place where a person had been.

She gave out with that, and it was long and deep and lonesome sounding.

It got quiet in the truck. And awful still.

And then she gave the death rattle again.

And then it was quiet in the truck.

Till she come out with that godawful noise again and it came to me she was snoring.

Chapter 35
Seven Hours After the Robbery

December 20, 1951
4:00 PM
Helen

Helen Mortimer clutched at the old GI overcoat and tried to close it as much as she could with the zipper broken as she sloshed across the snow-packed street, grateful for the rubber boots—an early Christmas present from the nuns at Saint Francis. Another gust of freezing wind and snow slapped her in the face as she got to the curb, and she pulled the olive-green wool-lined cap down tighter across her dark hair. She knew the hat made her look stupid. She resented the need for going out looking like this at all, but—

She bucked the wind as far as the Top Hat Bar and Grill and pushed open the worn oak door, then stopped for a second just inside, luxuriating in the warm, beery heat as her eyes adjusted to the darkness.

She scanned the room carefully.

He wasn't here.

Nothing but that damn Christmas music:

...Oh what fun it is to ride
In a one-horse open sleigh—hey!
Jingle Bells,
Jingle Bells....

Weary, weary from a lot more than just walking all over town through the snow on a day like this, she shambled over and leaned against the bar. The young-looking guy behind it served a martini to a well-dressed man, then smiled at her and came up to that end.

"Hiya, Helen." His smile was just a little crooked, but in the dim light behind the bar no one could see it was from a series of scars running down one side of his face. "Get you something?"

She tried to smile back at him—Fred was a sweet guy, and it wasn't his fault to come back from the war all banged up like he was—and then discovered she was just too tired to make the effort.

"You seen Mort?" she managed.

"Get you some coffee." Fred looked straight into her eyes, easy and untroubled, and she knew he hadn't seen Mort. She appreciated the coffee though, as he set the steaming cup on the bar and she warmed her hands on its sides.

"Now I think at it," he said slowly, "I might have seen him coming from Brother Sweetie's earlier today. He still wears that hat? The grey felt one?"

"I knew it." The crumb of hope seemed to nourish Helen and she took a sip of the hot coffee. "I knew he was tied up with that stinking fat mick."

"I don't know from him and Sweeney, Helen." Fred's smile was patient, almost loving. On the wall behind him there was a picture of the Bootheville Warriors varsity football team from 1940, and he was in it, somewhere well towards the back. And in the front right side was a teenage girl in a cheerleader outfit who looked a little like Helen.

"All I'm saying," he went on, "is I maybe saw Mort coming out of Brother Sweetie's this morning when I was out shoveling the sidewalk the first time. That's all."

"Yeah, Mort went out this morning early and said he had a job. Figured it was with that lousy mick."

"You ask Brother Sweetie?"

"Just now."

"So?"

"So that crooked Irish wouldn't talk straight if you paid him good money for it." She drank a big gulp of the coffee. "But just because I know he's lying doesn't mean I can make him tell the truth."

"Gee that's tough." Fred tried to look sympathetic, but not so much as to get pulled into anything that would put him up against Brother Sweetie. On careful consideration, he decided to steer the conversation elsewhere. "So what are you folks doing for Christmas?"

"I don't know." Helen finished the coffee, slowly, trying not let on it was all she'd had since breakfast. "It's for the kids, Christmas."

"That's right." Fred seemed glad to get the conversation back on safe ground and he wanted to anchor it there. "For the kids, that's right."

Helen thought about Mort's promise to come home with money. Thought about how New Year's they might have to move in with Mort's dad. Or try to. She reached reluctantly into her pocket to pay for the coffee.

"On the house," Fred waved her off. "I just happened to think, though…"

"Yeah?"

"I saw Howard over at the barbershop, he was just opening up."

"And so?"

"And so this time of year he's busy, everybody gets themselves spruced up for the holidays and all, and I remember I wondered how he come to be getting started so late, that's all."

"You figure he's seen Mort?"

"I don't know did he has or did he hasn't. I'm just saying he was late opening up, and that means he's been someplace around town—heck, all I know he visiting Santa Claus at Belkin's there—but maybe he's been around town today and he's maybe seen Mort is all I'm thinking."

The idea put new strength into Helen. She straightened up from the bar.

"I'll try it," she said. "Thanks a lot Fred." And she meant it.

"Anything for you, Helen," and he meant it too. "You know that. Merry Christmas if I don't see you."

But she was already out the door and the martini down at the other end needed attention.

Five minutes later and a block down the street, Helen looked in on Howard through the big glass window with the candy-cane stripes around it. Howard was paying careful attention as he shaved the back of a blonde man's neck. He looked up at her, then quickly away.

Too quickly.

She went in the shop.

Chapter 36
Seven Hours and Thirty Minutes
After the Robbery

December 20, 1951
4:30 PM
Walter and Eddie

We were still a good ways outside Bootheville when Walter finally moved around some and looked down at Callie snoring on the seat. He squirmed his legs under her bent knees, closing his eyes and sighing at the pain of it, then slowly, carefully, used his sleeve to wipe snot off his upper lip. Looked down again at Callie.

"Damn," he said, "don't somebody want to shut up that noise?"

"How you feeling?" I asked.

"It hurts some."

"Whereabouts and how?"

"My hands and feet mostly. Burns. And feels like you was standing on them."

"They say that's a good sign." I didn't know that for sure but it sounded reasonable, and it might make him feel better to think it.

"That's what I heard too." He pulled off his gloves with his teeth and held up his hands. I didn't much like the color of them but he could wiggle his fingers a little and I took that as another good sign.

"We got time for a cigarette?"

"Yeah, I guess so. I don't want to get us into Bootheville before dark anyway."

I found a wide place in the road that wasn't drifted over with snow and pulled over to park. Then I thought of that lunch box I threw back behind the seat when I loaded everyone up, and I fished around for it. Inside there was a piece of salt pork and a slab of cornbread wrapped in wax paper, and a thermos. I opened it and sniffed.

"Coffee," I said. "Here drink some. Not too much."

He got the thermos between his hands and I could see him wince with the pain of holding it, but he slopped a little into his mouth. Then I took a drink. It wasn't warm, but it was coffee and it felt good inside me and besides, right then I was about as hard to please as a hungry dog. I figured Walter couldn't hold meat in his fingers so I held it up to his face and he bit some off.

"Chew it slow," I said, "and chew it up good. We don't want none of us choking."

"That's facts," he said through the food. Then he just concentrated on getting it down and I took a bite off it myself while I broke him up a piece of cornbread and by then he was ready for me to feed it in his mouth.

That's how we ate, and when we finished I lit up a cigarette and took a long, good pull on it before I stuck it in his mouth. He took in a deep lungful and we filled the cab with smoke. I cracked a window.

"How you feeling now?" I asked.

"Better."

The look on his face when he tried moving around some told me different but no good arguing it with him, so I passed him back the cigarette for another deep drag. "Nothing like a smoke after a good meal."

"And that was nothing like a good meal," he finished. It wasn't funny, but both of us laughed.

"Soon as we get back to Brother Sweetie," I said, "we'll get somebody to look at your hands and feet."

Just that time Callie let out a snore that shook the windows on the truck. She swallowed something through her nose, tried to move, moaned with the hurt of it and started back in snoring again.

"What we going to do about her?" Walter asked me.

"Got to get her to a hospital," I said. "That sunuvabitch that shot at you opened her up a good one."

"I heard what she said."

"What's that?"

"What she said about how she knew you did the robbery. Likely knows I did too."

"Yeah, I guess she figured it out."

"So what we do about her?"

"Well, like I said, I was figuring to take her to Bootheville General and drop her in there and then get the hell out before anyone stops us too much."

"You figure she ain't gonna die?"

"Hope not."

"You figure she'll maybe come around and talk about us some?"

"Could be she will."

"Give out what we look like?"

"Give a description of us?" I took a long drag on the cigarette and let it out slow. "I guess it's likely she could."

"Do she talk, Brother Sweetie might get mad over it. Over us leaving her alive."

"Likely so, but nothing I can do about it." It was getting dark. I put the truck in gear and swung back out onto the road. In all the time we were stopped there no one had passed us either way. The snow was smooth and unbroken clear over to the lights from Bootheville, just a couple miles off.

"Well, you think we should do something...you know, to keep her from talking?"

"I've thought at it," I said, "and like I say, there's just nothing

I can do about it. I mean I can't just shoot her down in cold blood. Not a woman."

"Not even a woman ugly as her?"

"She sure ain't a pretty sight, is she?"

"Pretty?" he snorted. "Hurts my eyes just to look her way."

"Yeah, but she's a woman—"

"Look like the Russians are coming, is what she looks like."

"Yeah, I guess,"

She let out another snore on my lap.

"She make a blind man grateful."

"Like I said, I just don't figure I could shoot a woman," I said, "not even one looks as scary as her. Not when I'm clear-headed, anyway. I mean, was I mad at her or something, yeah, sure, I could kill her was I mad at her, or did she take a shot at me or something. But not cold-blooded and deliberate. Can't do it. Besides, she maybe saved my life back there."

"She did that?"

"Yeah, she come up to that guy that shot at you and put him off killing me."

"Yeah?"

"Yeah, and she give me the idea how to pull you up out of that car. So I figure, her being a woman and us maybe owing her something for helping out like she done…. Nope, I just can't kill her."

"I guess not."

I'd started seeing tracks in the snow and next thing we were driving past houses on our way into the city. A lot of them had those colored lights out for Christmas, strung up on the porch and around the windows. Now and then a car would crawl up the road at us and we even saw a snowplow limping along like a tired boxer waiting for the bell.

"Do you want to kill her, I won't stop you," I said. "I can't do it myself, Walter, but I ain't going to fight you for her."

He looked at her a long couple seconds. Listened to that ungodly noise she was making. Then, "My hands ain't well enough to shoot a gun I guess."

"We could put her out the car do you want to," I said, "I mean, like I told you, I can't do it myself. But does she bother you, I'll drive on out of the city and let you put her out and likely she'll freeze to death before anyone finds her."

"I guess not."

"You sure?"

"You gonna make me say it, ain't you?"

"Say what?"

"I guess I can't kill no woman neither. Even one as looks like that. And like you say, she maybe did us a good turn back there."

"So I guess we take her into the hospital?"

"It's getting dark enough, we should get it done easy and nobody seeing us too much."

"That's good," I said, "because we're just almost there now."

It was a couple short blocks through the downtown, all decked out in red and green bells, candy canes and silver tinsel, and the store windows all full of toys and nice clothes, flashing colored lights and what-all. I turned a corner to come up on the back of the hospital where they bring in the emergency cases.

And right there was every cop car in the world, just sitting there.

Chapter 37
Eight Hours and Thirty Minutes
After the Robbery

December 20, 1951
5:30 PM
Walter and Eddie

Well, hell.

Okay so it wasn't every cop car in the world; there was maybe only a half-dozen or so, from a couple different cities, the Sheriff's Office and the Highway Patrol—and no one in them that I could see. They were parked around an oversized tow-truck, and hanging off the back of that truck there was a big square boxy-looking thing that looked like an armored car in the gathering dark.

So they hadn't let any grass grow underfoot, that was sure, but they weren't exactly coming up behind us either. I just hadn't figured the cops to be throwing their party here at Bootheville General Hospital. Why the hell weren't they in Willisburg?

Then I remembered that guard I shot. They'd naturally want to get him to a hospital and likely his brother too, to get what details they could out of them while they got looked at. So they'd come to the closest hospital same as I had, and that landed us all here in Bootheville and Merry Christmas, everybody.

I eased the truck in past the cop cars and up to a big glass double-door where I hoped there'd be an orderly standing, but no such luck.

"Wait here." I eased my leg out from under Callie's head and she stopped her snoring long enough to moan up some, like a baby doll does when you lay it down. In the light from outside I could see Walter was gritting his teeth, wincing with the hurt from his hands and feet and trying not to show it too much. "Right back," I said to him. "Anybody comes out, make like you're hurt real bad."

"Won't be hard," he said.

Outside in the parking lot there was some kind of speaker thing turned on and playing

To save us all
From Satan's power
When we were gone astray,
Ohhhh tidings of co-om-fort and joy…

I walked through snow that had been plowed and salted and covered with ashes till it was just ankle-deep slush up to the emergency-room doors. They were those glass doors, the new kind like they had in stores, where you step on a rubber mat and the door swings open and hits you in the face. On the other side, about fifty feet down a hall, I could see a guy in a white uniform, likely an orderly or something—and most likely he was the guy I needed to get that Callie woman out of the truck and off my hands. But he was talking to somebody.

I stopped just short of stepping on the mat and took a good look at who he was talking to—I didn't want to go interrupting some cop and keep him from going about his duties. No sir, not me. The guy was wearing a trench coat and a battered hat with a wide, drooping brim, and I figured him for a plain-clothes detective at first. Then I saw he was short and skinny and wearing glasses thick as boot heels, so most likely he wasn't a cop at all, and I figured to chance it.

I stepped on the mat and the door swung open and they both turned to see what it was.

"Emergency out here." I said it loud, but not shouting. "Stretcher case!"

The guy in white said, "Stretcher case?" and the one in the trench coat said, "I'll help you."

Before he walked over he picked up a hefty camera with a flash on it big as an electric fan and slung it around his neck and as he came out the door I saw he had something pinned on his coat that said PRESS, and I know I said it before but it bears repeating:

Well, hell.

They both came out that door carrying a canvas stretcher, and while I wondered what to do next I opened up the passenger side of the truck and Walter fell out and landed in the dirty snow at their feet. He moaned as the guy in white tried to help him up, and I wondered was he was faking it like I told him or was he really bad hurt, trying to stand on his frozen feet. His knees started to buckle and I moved in to prop him up against the side of the truck—and to kind of block them from seeing all those money bags piled up in the bed. But I guess the hurt was too bad, and he was sure too heavy for me to hold, so he just sat down in the snow again.

The orderly took a look at him in the light from overhead. "Hey, we don't treat them here." And the reporter got a look on his face like he'd lost interest. That was fine with me as we weren't planning to stick here anyway.

"Not him," I said, "in the truck."

"The hell," the orderly said. He looked in the truck and saw the big bulky lump stretched along the seat. "What happened to this guy?"

"Not sure," I said, "she said she got shot."

"It's a woman?" The reporter woke up again, like he could see a story coming on. "Let's get her inside."

The orderly set one end of his stretcher against the edge of the seat and I held the far end while they got Callie's feet up on it and started easing her out, gently, along the axis of her body, pulling by the hem of her heavy coat to keep it from hanging up.

When they had her almost out on the stretcher the reporter looked my way. "What's your name, Officer? Where'd you find her? What happened?"

I almost said I was Officer Drapp, since I was getting used to it by now, but then I figured that him being a reporter he might have covered that murder of Gonzago case, and if he did, he'd know Drapp personal, so I said,

"Jack Tull. I'm Captain of the Citizen's Auxiliary, Piketon Police."

"Piketon?" I could see his opinion of me drop a notch when I said I wasn't a real cop, but just a jack-leg deputy from a toonerville town like Piketon. Meantime, they got Callie all the way out onto the stretcher and I tried to casually hand my end off to him but he went on, "Piketon in on this too?"

"Not really." I sort of nudged my end over to him again but he didn't take me up on it. "Chief wanted us to set up roadblocks as a precaution in case they came our way. That woman there, she drove up on me in this truck, driving crazy all over and I flagged her down and then I saw she was shot. Then I saw this feller inside near froze-up, but she was too bad hurt to tell me anything, they both was bad hurt like this and just almost passed out, so I radioed in and the chief said to get in the truck and take her here because with these roads the way they are they sure couldn't get a medic out to us, so I did like he said and I guess I'm here now."

He lost interest in me about halfway through all that and started blowing on his hands in the cold, which is what I was hoping. I made to hand him my end of the stretcher again, but the orderly said, "Let's get her inside."

"I'll just get a shot of the truck, be right in," the reporter said. Dammit.

And next thing I was carrying my end of that heavy stretcher —jeez, that woman weighed a ton!—into the hospital, down one hallway then another, past a bunch of cops hanging around, and the orderly decided he'd be helpful to the cops, so while we were rolling Callie onto a bed with wheels on it he called out, "This woman's been shot," and they all perked up good and came over.

Well, dammit again.

Time to ease away, get back out there, get Walter back in the truck and get us lost. I would have done it, too, but things just kept getting better and better. Right then the reporter runs in and yells to the cops standing around,

"Hey! Outside! It's the money from the robbery!"

Dammit, dammit, dammit.

There was a big rush for the back door, and me with my cop clothes I blended right in with the blue crowd and we all came out the door and around the truck. The reporter stayed inside; likely wanted to be the first to talk to the daring young lady who rescued all that money. I thought about what he'd do when they pulled back that hood Callie was wearing and he got a look at her, but that was somewhere off the back of my mind. Main thing I was thinking about was what the hell was I going to do now?

We got outside to the truck, and there was about six or eight of us I guess. I took a long breath when I saw Walter had crawled away and he was sitting up against a wall in a shadow by a vent blowing warm air. Don't know how he got himself there— couldn't have been easy work, not for a man with frozen hands and feet, but he'd done it and that made things a little less awful.

Which ain't saying much.

Me and all these cops crowded around the back of that truck while the music out there played,

...the horse knows the way
to carry the sleigh
O'er the white and drifting sno-oww,
Over the river
And through the woods...

and we stared at the money bags a while. Then everyone started talking, asking where'd the truck come from and who brought it here, and I played just as dumb as the rest of them, like I'd never seen that truck before in my life and it could have dropped from Mars for all I knew. Finally somebody in the crowd wearing stripes on his sleeves said, "I'll call the chief. You guys get that money inside."

So I backed off and just watched as a half-dozen cops picked up all those bags of money and carried them in the hospital.

Once they were all inside and nobody looking, I walked through the packed-down ice-slush over to Walter. He'd propped himself up a little more, but he still looked like Death on a rainy Monday morning, and I bent down to him.

"Walter," I said, "we got a job of work ahead of us."

Chapter 38
Eight Hours and Forty-Five Minutes
After the Robbery

December 20, 1951
5:45 PM
Eddie

"You wait here," I said, "I'm coming right back and get you inside."

"Wasn't going far anyhow," he managed.

I guess nowadays they keep wheelchairs handy by the hospital doors to help folks in and out, but back when I'm writing about that idea never struck anybody yet, so I had to look around inside a few minutes before I found one in a back room. And don't you know, just when I started wheeling it out, that orderly, the one that helped to get Callie in, he comes by, so I tried to look busy and official.

Didn't work, though.

"What you doing?" he asked.

"Man outside," I never broke my pace, "needs took care of."

"I told you outside, officer, we don't treat those Sambos here." He talked like a man who doesn't get to give orders very much, so when he can he wants to get the most out of it. "They got a place on Fourth Street you can take him there."

I just ignored him and kept moving, and hoped he wouldn't follow me out in the cold. That worked, anyway.

It was kind of a tough job out there, getting Walter up and into that wheelchair. Finally I bent over and had him lock his arms around my neck, then I straightened up, pulling him up with me, grabbed his belt through his coat and we danced around till I got him sat in the chair, while all the time that music was going,

> ….*make the Yuletide gay,*
> *From now on,*
> *Our troubles will be far awaaaay…*

"Don't forget to act sick," I said, unnecessaily.

I hand-hauled that wheelchair backwards through the snow-sleet gunk in the parking lot till we got to the dry place at the door. Then as we were coming in, that orderly pops up again.

"I told you he can't come in here." He moved in front of us, and I started calculating how it might be to kill him and stuff his body in one of the big trash cans outside. It sounded like too much work just now, so I just gave him the same look I gave those two guards on the armored car this morning and said,

"Find me a doctor."

For just a half split second he looked back at me like he was going to make a fuss out of this. Then he read the look in my eyes, gulped and went scuttling away and came back before long with somebody else.

I guess you never can tell, but I had my own ideas about the kind of doctor who ends up working on the late shift in a hospital, and it ain't a real high opinion. This one looked to be fifty maybe, with a belly that bounced into the hall ahead of him. His shoes were scuffed, and there was a mustard stain on his white coat. He took a short dainty puff on a filtered cigarette and flashed a smile at me that beamed like a dull thud. Then he looked down at Walter in the chair through smudgy wire-rim glasses. Before he could say anything the orderly who brought him here said, "I told him he couldn't come in, Doctor Robbins. I told him we don't treat them here."

"Well for snakes' sakes." His voice was soft and wheezy and kind of like the way a woman sings, but there was a soft chuckle somewhere in there as he looked down at Walter. "A black man wheeled into our sacrosanct white temple of healing. No doubt this must be a harbinger of the imminent collapse of civilization as we know it. And to think we are here to witness…"

He hunkered down, carefully flicking the ash off his cigarette onto the floor, pushing his belly up against Walter's knees, and squinted at him over the tops of his dirty glasses. "What's your story, sir?"

"Whububna mum," Walter said.

"Whububna mum," the doctor repeated. "Seems to be a lot of that going around." He looked close at the purple knot on Walter's forehead, kind of felt at it around the edges, then moved a finger side-to-side in front of his eyes. Looked up at me. "Perhaps you may shed some light?"

"All I know is he come in with some woman who got shot and he may know something on that armored-car robbery. We need to talk to him soon as we can, and that means taking care of him. Here. Now."

"By all means." Robbins struggled to his feet and held onto the arm of the wheelchair a second, like getting up got him dizzy. Took another puff on his cigarette. "Room C, I think."

He led us off, waddling in front on shoes run over at the heel, me pushing Walter behind in the chair and that orderly just almost dancing with how upset it made him. "…Doc Woodrum finds out," he was saying, "he finds out about this and I don't want no part of it. He asks me, I'll tell him I told you and I told *him* too." His voice covered me and Walter both like a bad smell.

Robbins stopped in his tracks and swiveled his belly around at him, and I saw the buttons on his white coat strain from the work. "Doctor Woodrum will learn of this when you run off and tell him, Alfred," he said, "which I expect will happen very shortly. And I shall face his disapproval as I have faced yours. For now, however, I think your services can be readily dispensed with here, and Godspeed to you."

He turned back and started leading us wherever we were going, except Alfred wasn't in the parade anymore.

"I'm afraid Alfred was correct," Robbins said back to me over his shoulder, "Doctor Woodrum holds some, ah, narrow views on whom we should treat in this facility, and I'm afraid he may become a bit difficult on the situation once he's apprised of it. So perhaps we should hurry."

We hadn't gone far when we got to a room that said "C" on the door and he showed us in like he owned the place.

"Ignore the examining table," he said, looking down at Walter again, "I believe you'll be more comfortable if you just stay there in the wheelchair." He locked the brakes on the chair. "Mister... uh…"

"Johnson," I said, "The ID in his wallet says he's Sam Johnson."

"And perfectly suited to this occasion." There was a stool on wheels and Robbins flicked it over with the toe of his shoe and parked his butt on it while it was still moving.

"I'm Officer Drapp," I said, "Willisburg Police." I figured to change things up a little, maybe slow folks here down some did they ever get around to comparing stories about this.

"I've heard of you, sir." Robbins rolled himself over to a white cabinet and opened a drawer. "I've heard good things spoken of you. The murder of Gonzago…."

He slipped a small bottle out of the drawer, uncorked it and took a short drink. Corked it back up and replaced it carefully, pulling some sterile white bandages over it before he shut the drawer again, "Yes sir, you have a reputation as a rather smart customer, Officer Drapp."

"Well, I don't want to get you in trouble, Doctor, but we may need to move this guy. And soon. You got something will kill the pain but won't knock him out?"

"The very thing." He sailed across the room on his stool to another cabinet and looked at it like he was scanning a shelf at the library. "There's Fentanyl, of course, but that can cause lethargy and confusion. Then there's….here."

He pulled himself off the stool and grabbed a bottle, then plunked back down and launched himself back to Walter.

"Acetaminophen." He shook four white tablets out of the bottle onto his fleshy pink palm. "The latest thing. Could you fetch this gentleman some water, Officer Drapp?"

I filled a paper cup from the sink and fetched it over. Robbins pushed the pills into Walter's mouth, then held the cup so he could grab it and wash them down. Some of the water dribbled down his chin but he got them in.

"What is that stuff?" I asked.

"A new high-potency pain reliever with approximately the same side-effects as aspirin," he held up the bottle, "and modestly effective as a hangover-preventative, though somewhat hard on the stomach."

"Mind do I try one?" I was starting to feel the effects of coming off that tower, where I'd used my back to break the fall. And the stiffness you get from a couple hours driving. And the places on my ribs and stomach where Scranton had shined the hard tip of his steel-toed boots, they didn't feel real good either.

"By all means." He shook out a couple pills for me. "Now just let me have another look here…"

I gulped the pills down with water while he swiveled over to Walter and gently started touching the swollen knot on his forehead where it hit the steering wheel, then his hands and cheeks. Just touched, didn't rub. Then asked, "Can you feel that, sir?"

Walter shot me a look over the doctor's shoulder, just to let me know he wasn't as knocked out as he sounded.

"Burns," he mumbled, "hands burn."

I turned and started looking close through the glass doors of that medicine cabinet.

"Head injury, that's obvious," Robbins said, "and frostbite as well, but only second-degree I think. It will be painful of course, with blistering of the skin, but I don't look for permanent damage…no signs of concussion…" He turned and tilted his head up at me just as I turned back from the medicine cabinet. "Is this man going to prison, Officer Drapp?"

"I got no way to know yet." That was true.

"See that he continues to get this for the pain." He passed the bottle of pills to me. "Prison is quite bad enough without it. Now have you time for me to soak his hands and feet in water?"

"Probably a good idea," I said, "but keep his shoes and socks close by. We may need to move him fast." Real fast, I was thinking, but I tried not to let on.

Robbins bent over—I could see the effort it cost him—and undid Walter's shoelaces. Eased his shoes and socks off real gentle.

"You going to get in trouble for this?" I turned back around to check that medicine cabinet again and this time I thought I saw what I was after. "For treating him here, I mean?"

He was already filling a couple metal bedpans with lukewarm water and sliding them under the footrests on that wheelchair. "Well, Doctor Woodrum will probably insist on burning whatever we've touched," he smiled at the notion, "but I rather think my personnel file will stand the strain of yet another entry. Should circumstances dictate, I will simply join the circus and hide my tears behind the mask of a clown."

I wondered was he was already doing it. "Okay to leave him here a while?" I asked. "I don't figure him to be going anyplace with his feet like that, but I don't want anyone else getting to him yet either. Not till he wakes up more anyway. And I got to go start tagging evidence. Might be gone a while."

"He should be fine right here." Robbins pinched his fleshy lower lip between his thumb and finger for a minute, figuring it over I guess. "Perhaps you should close the door, though. As a precaution."

"Fine."

Robbins was still bent over arranging the water pans, and I looked over his shoulder at Walter.

He shot me a wink.

About then I got to feeling the painkiller kick in, loosening up my arms, easing the hurt in my back and sides.

Time to get back to work, I guess.

"You got a doctors' room here?" I asked. "A place to wash up or something?"

"By every means," Robbins said, "just outside and down the hall: right-left, then left-right. Hmm, perhaps I should escort you…"

"Thanks a lot."

"And before we go, may I get you something else from our supplies there?" He didn't miss much, that Doc Robbins.

"I just saw… How about a couple Benzedrine tablets? Been kind of a long day."

"Benzedrine?" He didn't exactly make a face, but I could see he was thinking it. "Nasty stuff."

"They gave it to us back in the Army plenty enough," I said. "Kept us awake and moving when we had to be awake and moving."

"We did indeed." He looked like he was thinking back on something and didn't exactly like it. "Well, if you feel you know best, help yourself."

I knew what he meant. That stuff gets your heart going like

there was something inside your chest trying to kick its way out. And I knew some guys in the Army got so they couldn't get along without it. But that never stopped them handing it out to us when we couldn't get food or sleep, and right now I needed anything I could get. I took two tablets and washed them down with water.

"Thanks." I wiped water off my chin. "Now where's that Doctor's room"?

Chapter 39
Nine Hours After the Robbery

December 20, 1951
6:00 PM
Helen and Mort

In the alley behind Lola's Helen Mortimer looked down at the curled up, beer-soaked-and-bloody thing she called her husband. He looked like he was sobbing, and she wanted to bend down and take him in her arms, but she decided to be angry with him first.

"Christ–Jesus, Mort! Drunk again? You went out and got drunk, this is what you did?"

"Helen?" He looked up at her and clenched his teeth to try to hold the loosened ones in. He was long past shivering from the cold, long past even feeling it. "What you doing here?"

The pitiful sound of his voice broke her resolve and she bent down to hold him, shocked at first by the cold that seemed to radiate from his body, then angry again at the smell of beer all over his clothes.

"Jeez, Mort," she tried to make her voice hard, "Did you have to go out and get drunk again?"

"Didn't get drunk." There was something funny in his voice that she couldn't remember ever hearing there before. Something kind of scary.

"Bastard robbed me."

Helen gave up on being angry and tried to sound motherly. "I told you not to get into any deal with Brother Sweetie."

"Wasn't Brother—" Mort gulped something salty from his nose and he couldn't tell if it was mucous or blood. "That bastard Healey."

"You were in there with Boxer Healey?" She didn't have any trouble now being angry. "Mort, you gone stupid? Gambling with Boxer Healey? That man plays cards for his living; no wonder he beat you!"

"Didn't beat me." It was slowly rising up inside Mort now. He could feel it there in his gut, building and burning hotter, like something bitter and foul-tasting. He looked at his wife, trying to make her understand it. "Helen, I won!" He saw how crazy that sounded coming out his bloody mouth in the snow in a dark alley. "I won from him, Helen. I did, I beat him...." He had to make her see it. "Helen, it was four hundred dollars and I won it off him and—" He blinked suddenly. "How'd you find me? Where the hell am I anyhow?"

"You're back of Lola's." *Had he really won four hundred bucks? Off Boxer Healey?* "I been looking for you all day. Finally I got Howard at the barbershop to say he might've seen you by Lola's. My god, Mort, did you really win all that?"

"Where—where's the kids?"

"The Gomez girl across the hall, she's watching them." It was sweet of him, she thought, to worry about the kids. Just like him, too, to think about them when he was lying here beat to a pulp. She hugged him, strong and soft at the same time, and tried to will some heat from her body into his. "Can you get up?"

"Got to—" He struggled. Got one cold, unfeeling leg under him and made it push. Helen steadied him and he got the other one where he wanted it. She pulled and steadied him some more till he was something like standing up.

"—got to kill that bastard Healey," he finished.

"Don't talk crazy," Helen said, "you're going to the hospital."

"Can't afford no hospital," he said. "Got to kill him."

"We'll go to the clinic on Fourth." She was motherly again. "We want to get you well. For Christmas. For the kids."

"Ain't going to Christmas." His voice was flat and cold now, almost as cold as his hands. "Just don't plan on going that far. And I ain't going to no clinic. Gonna get me a gun and kill him."

"I said you're going to the clinic." Helen held him closer, partly to keep him from falling and partly just to hold him closer. "Can you walk to the corner?"

"Helen." He felt his teeth loosen as he tried to talk, and clenched them together again. Tried to talk without opening his mouth, tried to make her see it. "Helen he took four hundred dollars from me. Just took it like I was nothing. Like I wasn't a man or—or *nothing*! Like he was supposed to have it and like I—like I wasn't supposed to have *nothing*!"

"We'll talk about it later. We'll think what to do. Now lean up against me, we'll walk you to the street and catch a streetcar. Can you get that far?"

He walked. Because he had to. *Nothing else to do*, he told himself, *got to walk. But I got to make Helen see it, see how it is…*

"Helen," he managed the words, pushed them out from between his bleeding lips some way. "Helen he just took the money from me like he was *supposed* to do it!"

"I know, hon; you said it already. And look, we're to the street now. Jeez, ain't there no streetcars running in this snow? Walk with me, hon…."

"Helen, he didn't even use his fists. Just slapped me open-hand, like I wasn't even good enough to use his fists on!"

"Just keep walking, hon. We'll get you home and you can rest and we'll talk."

She doesn't get it. Doesn't see why I have to kill him. He tried not to put so much weight on her, tried to do more walking on his own, but he just hurt too much for it. And he tried to think. *Can't take him with my fists, that's sure.*

"Gonna get a gun." Mort noted with surprise that he was talking out loud, still with his teeth clenched. "Get a gun and kill 'im."

"You listen to me." She got her arms tight around his reedy body, held him as hard as she could, and kept walking him through the snow, one eye out for a streetcar, a taxi cab, maybe a black-and-white…no, they'd ask too many questions. Just keep him moving and, "Listen to me, Mort. You are not killing nobody. Nobody, you hear me?"

"The money. We needed it and he just—just *took* it!"

"Your kids are not going to wake up Christmas morning and their daddy in jail for murder. You hear me, Mort? I am not going to let that happen. Not to them and not to you. You understand me?"

He said nothing and she settled for it and kept walking him up the snowy sidewalk. *Never figured on anything like this,* she thought. *Hell, you find you a guy and stand up there and say "I do" and you never see it coming, nothing like this anyhow. Who'd figure little Helen the cheerleader to be carrying her husband up the street in the snow, and him all bloody and beat up like…like….*

She held him even tighter. Felt tears welling up and refused to show them.

Kept walking.

They were just a block or so from home when his knees rubbered and he went down, almost pulling her with him as he sat in the snow in a crumpled heap.

"Gawwwd…" It came from him like air out from a punctured football, leaving him all empty inside—beaten and empty. "Helen, I—I got to have something. Something warm. Inside, I got to have something…so cold…."

"We're almost home, hon." She reached down to pull him up, but it was like an armload of wet wash; he kept slipping, down into the snow. "C'mon, get up...."

"Can't," he managed, "gotta...Helen, get me something hot. Please, Helen..."

There was a diner across the street. Brightly lit and looked full of people stuck there by the snow. "Right over here, Hon," she urged, "just get up and come on."

"I can't," he said again, "I just can't go in there looking like—" his voice trailed off once more. "Bring me something. Anything? So cold...."

She left him there and started across the street, her cheap rubber overshoes squeaking and squelching in the wet half-packed snow that buried sidewalk, pavement and curb.

Helen blinked a second in the bright lights inside the diner. It felt warm there, and she let herself enjoy it while her eyes adjusted. *Damn, it's crowded in here!*

She pushed toward the counter to order coffee to go. There was a man in front of her holding three checks. And a man in front of him, hugging four take-out bags, fumbling to get at his wallet under his overcoat. And a woman in front of him, carefully scanning the dessert case, her eyes going from the cherry pie to the coconut cake, to the rice pudding...now back to the cherry pie....

He needs me. Mort needs something hot. And he needs it now!

Helen fished into the pocket of her overcoat, ruffled her fingers past the half-stick of gum, the lipstick, the bobby pin, and through the few coins there, finally coming up with a worn Mercury dime. She stalked over to a middle-aged, well-dressed man reading the local paper overtop the meatloaf special. She plunked her dime down on the shiny-topped table, picked up his coffee, saucer and all, placed the saucer carefully over the mouth of the steaming cup and walked out, ignoring his goggle-eyed stare and the eyes of the other diners.

Got to get it to him. Hurry, now, he needs it bad.

Somehow she managed her way across the treacherous street. But Mort was gone.

She looked down the street for a long moment, then back at the place in the snow where she'd left him. Found his tracks and followed them up the sidewalk about a half-block, then lost them when they crossed the street. She remembered him lying there, bloody, beer-soaked and shivering, and the words seemed to shape themselves in her mind:

I'll find that lousy sunuvabitch I married and kill him myself.

Chapter 40
Nine Hours and Twenty Minutes
After the Robbery

December 20, 1951
6:20 PM
Eddie

Robbins led me down a mess of halls, all painted light green or skin-colored till we finally got to where a door said NO ADMITTANCE and he pulled out a mess of keys on a chain and found the one to unlock it. It was a white-looking place: shiny white walls, white-tile floors, white lights and sinks. I blinked for a minute and took it all in. Then as I started over to a sink, there was this loudspeaker in the room and it came out with some fuzzy noise. All I could make out was something sounded like, "...Robbins get in my office damn quick."

He gave the loudspeaker kind of a surly look, pried a little box out of his pocket and shook some Sen-Sen flakes onto his pillow-soft hand.

"Have some?" He waved the little box my way.

"No thanks," I said, "they taste too much like soap for me."

"They do indeed." He popped them in his mouth and looked at me over his glasses. "But the wages of gin is breath."

The loudspeaker on the wall barked again and he almost jumped.

"The wheels of justice," he pronounced, "generally grind much slower than this. You must have really stirred things up,

Officer Drapp. Until later then…" And he waddled out and down the hall.

Which was fine with me. I went over to the sink and rooted around in the mirrored medicine cabinet overhead till I found some cold cream and a razor. Then I stripped to the waist, rubbed warm water over my chest and back and toweled off with one of the stark-white towels stacked to one side. While I did, I looked in the mirror at the big ugly bruises that Scranton guy left there with his hiking boots, and I'm here to say they was big and they was ugly. I felt around my rib cage and told myself I didn't have nothing broken very much. Good enough. And whatever was in that pain medicine was picking me up some.

I lathered cold cream on my face and shaved close, not so much because I needed it but because I wanted to look sharp. Then I rooted around in a bank of lockers till I found a white shirt that almost fit me. I put it on, tucked it in straight, then brushed off my blue uniform pants with a towel and went to shine my boots with cold cream.

That's when I saw the hole there. In my boot, where Scranton had shot it.

I wondered how easy it was to notice, whether I could pass it off or something, but I could see quick that was no good. I looked around some more till I found a decent-looking pair of shoes someone had set to dry by a radiator. They were kind of loose, but good enough when I stuffed toilet paper in them.

I knotted my black uniform necktie back on, checking myself in the mirror.

I looked sharp. And ready to get that money back. The only thing stopping me now was about a dozen cops and one reporter hanging around the place.

I hunted around till I found a trench coat that fit good and a hat a little too big for me but it'd do. I stuffed some more toilet paper in the rim till it stayed up, then buttoned up the coat and looked in a mirror again.

What I saw looked enough like a plain-clothes cop to scare me. I took the badge off my police coat and pinned it inside my wallet then tucked it in the left-hand pocket of the trench coat. In my right-hand pocket I put the gun from my holster. Then I gathered up what was left from my cop clothes and shoved them down a big trash can under a pile of wet paper towels.

One last stop to wipe down anyplace where I might have left fingerprints, and then I marched out of there just like I knew what I was doing.

Out in the lobby, I stopped at a cigarette machine, put in a nickel and got myself a pack of Luckies. Peeled open the top and tapped one out as I walked over to a row of shiny wood-and-glass phone booths. Went inside one and dropped a dime in the slot. I had just enough time to light up and get in a good deep drag off it before I heard Brother Sweetie on the other end.

"Bud Sweeney's Used Cars," he rasped.

"Hiya, Brother," I said.

"It's Mister Sweeney to guys what owes me, and that's you mister, and where the hell are you anyhow?"

"Don't sweat it," I said, "not too much anyway. I'm at the public phones at Bootheville General Hospital."

"Hospital? What the hell you hanging around the hospital for?"

I liked how he showed concern. "We got bothered," I said.

"Wha'dya, kill somebody?"

"Not so's it shows," I said. "Walter got banged up some. I got to get him out of the hospital here before we get back to you."

"The hell with him." Even over the phone I could see the look on his face. It wasn't pretty. "Where's my goods?"

"It's a work in progress," I said.

"The hell's that mean?"

"Just something I heard a lady say today," I said. "It means we ain't done yet and maybe never will be. But if we make it, me and Walter are gonna need someone to meet us someplace with a big car or a small truck. Something big enough to carry all those bags. And it better be something I can recognize. You still got that ice truck in the garage?"

"I got it."

"Well get somebody to drive it out to…" I thought a minute. "You know Dell's Truck Stop between Bootheville and the Piketon bypass?"

"Yeah?"

"Have them meet me there. In the ice truck. And tell whoever you send I don't know what I'll be driving. Could be a cop car, so don't panic, do they see one pull right up to them."

"Where the hell am I going to find someone to drive out to Dell's on a night like this?"

"Use your personality," I said. "Or come yourself."

"What's the matter, I don't look busy here this close to Christmas?"

"Look, you want it or don't you?"

"Don't ask. Just get it there."

"And you just get that truck out to Dell's. Turn on the charm do you have to, but get it there."

"So I turn on the charm."

"See you after a while," I said, "and Merry Christmas."

I missed his answer as I hung up the phone.

Out in the lobby some of the cops had started to wonder what they were doing here, and the smart ones had figured they were better off in a warm dry hospital than outside on a night like this, so they were trying hard to look like they was busy at something important. As I passed through, I heard someone with stripes ask, "Where the hell's that deputy from Piketon?" but I paid him no mind.

Back in the part of the hospital where they do the operating there was a little place where they kept things organized; just a wide spot in the hallway with some hanging files and a wood table with a phone on it. Across from that there was a door with a cop standing outside it and a look on his face said *I'm guarding something*, which I figured meant the money was close by. I walked up to him and saw he was a Bootheville cop, so I kept going like I was about to walk right through him but when I got close I pulled the wallet out of my pocket and flashed the badge at him real quick.

"Officer Drapp," I introduced myself, "Willisburg Police."

Only he didn't pick up on it. He just nodded behind him and said, "He's in there—" and right then the door opens "—oh here he is now."

And out through that door comes a short, broad-shouldered guy wearing a Willisburg Police uniform and a mean look, and they both fit him pretty good.

And right next to him the big guard from the armored car— the one that I shot his brother.

Chapter 41
Ten Hours After the Robbery

December 20, 1951
7:00 PM
Eddie

The cop who was at the door smiled at me and said real helpful-like, "This here's Officer Drapp!" But Drapp just said, "Busy now," and brushed right past me to the phone on the table, which left me standing there staring at the guard from the armored car.

And him staring at me.

Everything I had, I put it in my eyes. Didn't show nothing on my face, just looked right back at him. And while I was at it, I slid my right hand in my coat pocket and let him see the outline of the gun there.

He recognized me all right. That was the first thing I saw on his big red face. Next thing I saw was that he didn't believe it, just couldn't get his mind around how I could be standing here in a building full of cops, staring him down. His eyes locked on mine, but I could see another part of him was checking to see was he still here on planet Earth or was he maybe just having a nightmare—and hoping he'd wake up from it quick.

And I kept staring straight on, my eyes walking right over him.

Behind me, Drapp was talking on the phone. He'd got the hospital switchboard operator to connect him with a cop shop and the way he was talking, it was to someone he knew.

"Bernie, put this out to the streetcars and roadblocks, then call the county with it, then Highway Patrol, then the local departments out fifty miles. And then the radio stations. Got that? I said first the county, then the patrol…yeah, then the local departments and then the radio. Ready? We're looking for an ambulance. White with a red cross. No, that's all I got—" He shot a look at the armored-car guard, the kind of look you give your kid when he brings home a bad grade card. It didn't do much good, since the guard was still looking goggled-eyed at me. "Only got a description on one of them," Drapp went on, "male, white, short, blonde and dressed like a doctor…. Well, I guess that means he's wearing white…. No, that's all we got." He looked at the guard again. "No, that's all we got. No, that's—hey, when I say *that's all we got* what does that convey to you? Okay. Anything doing out there? I didn't think so. No, I'll get back if there's anything. Yeah, Merry Christmas."

All the time he was talking I just kept my eyes on that guard, staring at him like he was the one should be worried, not me.

And he was worried. Could be it was hearing Drapp put out the description I'd fed him, which didn't look a bit like me, and it kind of made him out a liar. But there was something else on his mind, and I could see it coming up in his eyes while he tried to figure this out: here he'd been robbed by a guy who looked like a cop, and now here was the same guy looking right at him in a room full of other guys dressed like cops. He was figuring maybe the whole stick-up was a cop show. Maybe he was surrounded by the men that robbed him. Maybe….

His eyes broke away from mine and dropped to the floor, just in time for Officer Drapp to hang up the phone and turn to me with, "Yeah? You need me for something?"

I flipped open my wallet with the badge pinned in it, and I held it open so Drapp could get a good look. Only I didn't give him the chance; I jerked my head just a fraction toward that armored-car guard and pitched my voice low, like I was sharing a secret.

"Agent George Arliss, FBI." I put the wallet back in my coat, then nodded down the hall. "Can we step over here a minute?"

"Wondered when you guys were going to get here." Drapp followed me about a dozen steps away, and I made a show of positioning myself so I could talk to him and still keep an eye on the guard. "That guy back there," I said, "dressed as a guard. What did he give his name as?"

"Him?" Drapp started to look back over his shoulder, then checked himself. "Says his name's Logan Pierce."

"Not Larry Price?"

"No, Logan Pierce. Why?"

"Not Lawrence Piersall?"

"Not as far as I know. Just Logan Pierce, unless you know him by some other name."

"I'm not sure," I said. "He looks like a guy I saw a while back in Dayton. Only he had a moustache then. Called himself Lonny Pressman."

"How'd you come to know him?"

"Armored-car job."

I said it slow and looked at him all important-like. Pulled out my cigarettes and offered him one. As we both lit up, he took time for a casual glance behind him, and the guy from the armored car looked back at us both and shifted his feet like he was standing on something hot.

"And you think this is the same guy?" Drapp took a deep drag on his cigarette, breathed the smoke out through his nose, and turned back to me, talking low-voiced.

"Can't be sure," I said, "I need to get back to the office and check a few reports. Maybe I'm wrong but…"

"But he could be in on this?"

"Could be." I leaned on the wall, real casual, and Drapp did likewise. We were badge-brothers now, sharing trade secrets. "Kind of looks that way, but I can't say for sure. Not yet."

"The other one got wounded out there," Drapp said, "but it wasn't serious. Maybe they just did it to—"

"Wounded, you say?"

"Yeah, that means something to you?"

"Last two jobs this Larry Price pulled, one of the guards got a minor wound. In the head." I looked at Drapp like he'd handed me a cup of diamonds and Drapp looked back at me like I'd just turned on the lights.

"Yeah," he said, "they shot his ear off!"

"Like I said," I went on, "this may not be the same guy. I could be way off here, so we don't arrest him now. At least I wouldn't, was I—if I were you. Not yet. I just wonder... I don't suppose you could get us some fingerprints, could you?"

"Pierce's prints, you mean?"

"It'd be a big help," I said. "Like I say, we might not need them at all, I could be way off on this. But I won't know till I get back to the office, and even then, sometimes if the mug shots are close but not quite... You know what I mean?"

"Yeah." He took a thoughtful drag on his cigarette. "That could get kind of complicated, might have to book him on suspicion..."

"I don't want you getting yourself in trouble over it." I'd waved the bait at him long enough; time to start pulling in the string. "I mean, if it turns out this Pierce guy is actually Pressman, no one would blame you if he got away. I mean, not when we got the money back and all...."

That's all it took. Drapp got this look on his face like a fish snapping his jaw shut.

"I think we can do it." He waved over the cop who'd been

standing outside the door and said he should ask that guy from
the armored car there real nice to step back in the room he'd
been in and just relax for a few minutes. And that's how I got
rid of that guard and the extra cop.

So it was just me and Drapp there in the hallway.

"We appreciate your help." I tried to say it like there was the
whole FBI, Harry Truman and the United States Government
standing behind me. "Of course," I added quick-like, "we're
actually just trying to help out here. You folks are running the
show; the Office just sent me down to process the money."

Local cops don't hear much from the feds, and when they
do, it's usually talking down to them like a bunch of hillbillies.
And now here was me, a real Federal Man, telling Drapp he
was running things and asking could I help. And he ate it up
with a spoon. A big spoon, too,

"Process the money?" he asked.

"Oh yes," I said, "we need to get everything to the nearest
local police station for inventory and crime analysis. I don't
suppose you could arrange transport, could you?"

Chapter 42
Ten Hours After the Robbery

December 20, 1951
7:00 PM
Brother Sweetie

Bud Sweeney hung up the phone, swearing softly at the deepening snow, at Eddie, Walter, everyone he'd ever trusted with a job in his life, and the human race in general. He looked out in the lot. Just a young couple, the ones who'd been in here twice before, circling around a ten-year-old Nash, opening the doors and checking the tires, then testing the bumper, then opening the doors again....

Sweeney hustled his bulky mass outside. "Closing up folks." He took the door handle right out of the young man's hand, locked it and then slammed it shut. "Come back again, though."

"We were just wondering—" the man started.

"Not tonight," Sweeney said. "That was my mother just called, dying in the hospital and she wants a hot-water bottle. Understand it?" He started walking away even as he said it. The young man started to argue, saw the purposeful stride in the big man's body and decided to take their dreams elsewhere.

Sweeney never noticed. He was back inside the office, switching off the lights in the parking lot and flipping a switch behind him to kill the music, thinking about how he had to get the truck out to Dell's and wondering about Slimmy and if he was still waiting out there on Highway 12.

Right on cue, the phone rang again.

"Mister Sweeney?"

It was Sarge on the other end.

"Whaddaya got, Sarge, I'm kind of busy."

"I got Slimmy here, is what I got. He's kind of drunk. Even for Slimmy he's kind of drunk. And he's talking."

"Talking?" Sweeney's hand tightened around the phone receiver. "Talking about what?"

"I'm being real careful not to listen," Sarge said. Then, "I'm being real careful not to hear anything."

"How long's he been there?"

"That's funny too; some cop dropped him off here about one."

"A cop dropped him off?"

"Yeah, just let him out outside and then took off. I mean he took off fast as he could in this mess, the cop did. And then Slimmy comes in and he was already kind of drunk so I give him a sandwich, and he has a few beers, then a few more and now—well he's getting kind of loud."

Sweeney calculated. If Slimmy had blabbed anything to the cop, he wouldn't have just dropped him off there drunk. And Sarge said the cop took off in a hurry, right around one, which would be when they'd started looking for the Ajax truck. "Anybody else there?"

"A night like this? The only one else here is Joe and I told him to stay in the kitchen."

"Good work."

"Well, I owe you."

"Come June we'll see about fixing you up with that air conditioning thing you been talking about," Sweeney said. "Right now, I want you to slip him one—Slimmy, I mean—I want you to slip him one, and when he passes out you set him outside for me."

"Outside?" Sarge's voice got a little high and thin.

"Do I mumble?"

"This weather?"

"We got a bad line or something?"

"No, I hear ya. Just...." Sarge didn't want to go on and Sweeney didn't pick up the thought. They both just let it hang there between them on the telephone line.

"I'll be there when I can. May be a while. Probably better if you and Joe just close up and go on home."

"We were thinking on just sleeping here tonight, it's so bad out and all...."

"Sleep in the outhouse if you want to," Sweeney said patiently, "or at the Ritz. I don't really care where you are, just don't be there outside when I pick up Slimmy. Understand it?"

"Got it."

"I was hoping you had."

"Well...." Sarge wanted to end the conversation, but he felt that was Sweeney's call. "If I don't see you, Merry Christ—"

Sweeney hung up. He picked up a ring of keys from his desk drawer, right next to the snub-nose Colt .38 he kept there for social occasions, considered packing the .38 but decided against it. *The day I need a rod to settle anything like Slimmy...*

He walked out into the garage. Yeah, the ice truck was there, and ready to run. He looked up at the big black-and-white clock on the wall. After seven, way after. Nearer seven-thirty. And he had to get out to Dell's. And then clear the other side of the county over to Sarge's. Damn. Damn the weather.

There just wasn't enough time.

He heard something from back out in the office, and from a lifetime of experience knew it was something someone didn't want him to hear. Softly, surprisingly quiet for a man his size, he eased back to the doorway looking into his office.

Mort was standing there, bent over Sweeney's desk drawer, and holding the snub-nose Colt.

Chapter 43
Ten Hours and Thirty Minutes
After the Robbery

December 20, 1951
7:30 PM
Eddie

I couldn't give Drapp too much time. Did he get a chance to think it out, a smart guy like him, he'd start asking more questions, and they'd be hard ones, too. So while he was lining up how to move out that money, I was heading back to where I stowed Walter.

And running up to more trouble.

As I come down the hall to that room where I left Walter, I heard voices. Or one voice, really, high-pitched and sharp, and it didn't sound real happy. Inside I saw Walter, still sitting there looking three-fourths gone to Canaan, and Doc Robbins standing to one side, acting real sorry about all this. And leaning over Walter there's a tall guy in a clean, starched white coat, asking how comes he to be there anyway.

"Why didn't they send you to the clinic?" The doctor—the clean doctor, I mean, he was asking it, not Doc Robbins—he stepped around those water tubs where Walter was soaking his bare feet, leaned down to put a thumb under his left eyebrow —none too gentle, either—and pried his eye open. "Come on, boy, I can tell you're not passed out. You can't fool a white man with that—"

That's when Robbins saw me come in. He took in my new

outfit and blinked, and for a minute I thought maybe he wouldn't recognize me, but then up he pipes, "Uh—perhaps, uh, Officer Drapp here can explain it better than I could?" He gave me what they call a meaningful glance and said a little louder, "This is Doctor Woodrum, Officer Drapp."

The other doctor turned to me. Then back to Robbins. "Robbins you idiot, this isn't Officer Drapp." He turned back to me. "You're not Officer Drapp,"

"If you say so," I smiled at him, "I won't argue it with you. But this man's getting treated. Here. In your hospital."

"We don't treat them here." Woodrum sounded like another one of these guys that just loves the sound of himself giving orders. "That's our policy."

"Looks to me like you're treating him now." I looked at Walter. He was slowly, quietly pulling his hands out of the buckets of warm water. "Hell, you've treated him already."

Woodrum never took his eyes off me. Never saw Walter lift his feet from the water buckets in front of the wheelchair he was sitting in and put them gently down on a towel on the floor in front of him. Woodrum just looked at me closer. "Officer, I want your correct name and badge number. I won't have this attitude!"

"I won't charge much for it," I said.

Because while Woodrum was talking, Walter sitting there behind him, he reached down on the floor and slipped his hand into one of his empty shoes and then he stood up. I could see him wince with the pain of moving, but he did it, and then he tapped Woodrum on the shoulder, real gentle.

Woodrum got a look on his face like he wasn't used to getting interrupted when he was laying down the law at somebody, and then he turned around and saw Walter standing behind him. I didn't see the look on his face then, but his shoulders twitched in surprise as he faced Walter for about a second and a half.

"I hate to hit a man from behind," Walter said.

Then he swung the fist inside that heavy shoe of his and caught Woodrum right upside the head.

Woodrum, he fell sideways toward the cabinets, and he went to crumpling up while he got there. I watched him land, and he hit like in a movie I saw once where a plane crashed across the deck of an aircraft carrier—just all over the place like that. I looked over at Doc Robbins, and he was looking across the room to where his boss-doctor was lying there now like a pile of clean white laundry over in the corner.

Walter can swing a good one, does he want to.

Right now though, he just collapsed back to sit-down, near crying with the pain in his hands and feet. I turned to Robbins.

"You saw it," I said, "your Doctor Woodrum there slipped in the water and came down on his head. Didn't he?"

Robbins, from what I'd seen of him, I figured he was a man liked to talk. But he just kind of stood there looking at me, at Walter and then over at the pile of doctor in the corner.

Well, I didn't have time to use up a lot of words on him. I stepped up close to him and shot him the same look I gave that armored-car guard. "Give me your wallet," I said.

He blinked. I thought to slap him upside his fat face, but then I figured to hold off on that if I could.

"Give me your wallet," I said again, and I said it different this time. A lot different. Still nothing from Robbins but an empty stare, like he figured he'd wake up just any time now and things would make sense again. I just put a hand on his shoulder and squeezed some—real friendly, but I put a little hurt in it.

"Give me your wallet." It was the last time I was going to say it. And it was the last time I had to, because he finally woke up and dug in his back pocket and come up with an old brown leather thing with most all the skin wore off it.

I took it from him as he was bringing it around, just jerked it out of his hand and went through it fast. Come up with his driver's license.

"You still live over on Quincy?" I asked him.

"Uh—" he couldn't get the question at first. Then, "Yes. I live overtop Jake's place." He said it fast, but not too fast, and I was glad of that because it showed me he wasn't lying. Probably.

"Kind of noisy there, ain't it?" I asked.

"Well—I guess." He couldn't figure out where any of this was headed to, and the look on his face it was a little like a picture I saw once of Alice in Wonderland, all wide-eyed and what-the-hell. "But it's, um, convenient."

"Good," I said, "I like that you live someplace convenient. It's real good for you." I squeezed the license back in his wallet and stuck it back in his pocket. "Just remember I know where it's at."

He figured it out. And it woke him up.

"Now this man," I pointed down to Walter, "he's an important witness and he's your patient, and you got to get him ready to travel. Understand?"

"Perfectly," he said, "this man is my patient and—"

"And he's got to be ready to move out. And soon." I stood close and spoke soft, and I put my hand back on Robbins' shoulder, just to kind of remind him. "So you're going to get him ready to go. He's going to need bandages, those thick kind, on his hands and feet. Put his coat back on him first. And maybe slip him some more of those pills for the pain. And find some rubbers, some galoshes or something, to go on over his feet after you bandage them up. You listening?"

"Absolutely. I'm to bandage him and—"

"You put his coat on him first, that way you don't get trouble from the hand bandages. Then once you get his feet wrapped—what do you do then?"

"Then I find a pair of overshoes big enough to put on over the bandages."

"Right as sunshine." I gave him a smile, sort of. "Then you put him in that wheelchair and you take him out back to where that glass door is by the parking lot where all the cop cars are parked. And you wait there with him—wait inside there where it's nice and warm, understand—and I'll be there right along. You still with me?"

"Completely." And he was, he was really with me now. Something about the situation it struck him funny and exciting, like he'd got past trying to make sense of things and now he was just kind of going along for the nice ride and kind of tickled to think of his boss getting clocked out by a black man.

Made me glad I hadn't hit him.

"This man is my patient," he said it again, like he meant it, "and I shall have him ready for travel in ten minutes or less. Is there anything further, Officer?"

Yeah, I thought, *go through the phone book and find me a cheap lawyer for when this whole thing falls apart*. But I just said, "I'll see you around back."

I headed out. One more stop to make before I met up with Drapp and collected the money.

Chapter 44
Ten Hours and Thirty-Five Minutes
After the Robbery

December 20, 1951
7:35 PM
Brother Sweetie and Mort

"Boxer kept playing?" Sweeney was trying to get the story straight. "He played cards some more after you won the fifty? Didn't act mad and kick you out?"

"Played cards and lost. And then he robbed me. Just took it all, took everything I won." Like with Helen, Mort couldn't get it across to Sweeney. He couldn't put it into words, about being treated like nothing, and how Boxer never even used his fists. "I got to kill him," he said simply, raising the .38 for emphasis. "And you better not try to stop me."

Sweeney thought for a moment about reaching over, taking the gun from Mort's sweaty hand and clouting him over the head with it. Then changed his mind as an idea began to form. "Wouldn't think of stopping you," he said. "Wouldn't even think of trying. You kill Boxer or he kills you, it ain't no skin off my ass either way."

"Okay then."

"But I got a better idea."

"Don't try to stop me."

"Hell, go ahead. I was just thinking it might be a good thing to get your money back off him first before you go killing anybody. Might be a good thing for the wife and kids to have some spending dough, what with you getting your butt thrown in the clink for murder and all."

Another voice came from the doorway behind Mort. "Don't go dragging me and the kids into it, you lousy mick."

Mort spun around. Helen was in the doorway, sagging, out of breath and mad like he'd never seen her before: quiet-mad, not yelling or hitting, just real quiet. And real mad. Mort spun back to cover Sweeney again, but Sweeney was nowhere near him, just standing easy on the other side of the room.

"Well howdy, ma'am," he said, and smiled at Helen, "I hope you'll pardon my crude language. Didn't realize a lady was present here."

"Put it in a can," she said. "Just put that kind of sweet talk in a can and set it on the shelf. I told Mort he shouldn't go and get himself mixed up with a cheap crook like you, and now look what—"

"Helen I never—" Mort started.

"Yeah, this morning you said you wasn't going to do anything against the law, you said. Just going to do a little job for Brother Sweetie here and get fifty bucks. And I told you not to get mixed up with a lousy crook like him and now look: he's got you getting yourself robbed and ready to go kill somebody."

Mort started to answer but Sweeney jumped in.

"And I was just telling Mort I'd give him his money back and get Boxer to apologize, without killing nobody. No need to go killing anyone at Christmas is there?"

"Apology ain't enough," Mort insisted, "and money ain't enough, either. Not after how he treated me."

"Wait a minute," Helen said. She brushed past her husband and up to Sweeney, ignoring the gun, her eyes still hard, but now starting to soften with interest. "You'll get our money back?"

"Hell, I'll give it to you now. Out of my own pocket."

"Watch that language in front of Helen." Mort waved the gun that was beginning to seem increasingly irrelevant, even to him.

"I do beg your pardon, ma'am, but a man like me consorts sometimes with low company, and I grow careless in my speech." He turned back to Mort. "You want to go kill Boxer, that's your business. Understand it? Go ahead, blow his black head off, and while you're there tell him I wish him Merry Christmas and Happy New Year. All I'm saying is I can get you that four hundred back—double it if you say so—and I'll get Boxer Healey to go down on his knees and apologize to you in front of everybody. And he'll do it sincere, too. And when he sees you in the street from now on, he'll tip his hat. And call you Mister."

"He will?"

"I'll see he does. And I'll give you your money right now tonight."

"Well…." Mort lowered the gun.

"All I need is for you to do one little job for me—"

"That's it," Helen interrupted. "Mort you take that gun and walk downtown and kill Boxer. Whatever happens, it'll be less grief for all of us than you getting mixed up any more with this crooked mick."

Mort looked at Helen to see if she was joking.

"Helen, you wound me deeply." Sweeney tried smiling at her. "All I have in mind is about an hour's work, easy done and strictly legal." He turned back to Mort, deciding honesty was the best policy, or at least the only choice since he hadn't had time to come up with a good enough lie. "I need it done right quick and you're the only one can do it for me. You're important to me now, Mort. You're probably the only man I could find tonight who ain't wanted someplace, ain't got a record and can stand still if a cop walks right up to him. I need you. Understand it?"

"Need him to do what exactly?"

"Just take that ice truck back there and drive up to Dell's. You know Dell's, don't you, Mort?"

"Up by the Piketon bypass?"

"Sure. Just take that ice truck up there and wait for Eddie."

"That's all?" Helen asked, knowing it wasn't, not even anything close to it.

"That's all there is to it. Eddie's going to drive up and load something into the truck and then you can either ride back here with him or—" He almost said "or go to hell" but caught himself in time. "—or whatever you want."

"Sounds simple," Mort said. "Now what makes it worth so much to you?"

"And why can only Mort do it?" Helen put in.

"Well now, Eddie may be driving a police car. Or something like it, that's what he told me." Sweeney looked straight at Mort, like a general looks at his troops when he wants to impress them with their own guts. "And you're the only guy I know right this minute who can stand there and look innocent if a cop walks up and asks him his business."

"He *is* innocent, you cheap crook."

"Just what I meant to say," Sweeney put in quickly. "Now what do *you* say, Mort? You want that eight hundred, or you want to go kill Boxer?"

"Make it a thousand," Mort said.

"Eight hundred," Sweeney said firmly, "and I'll give it to you now this minute."

"No." Mort shook his head, winced from the pain and squeezed his eyes shut to clear his vision. "You give it to Helen." He turned to his wife. "Honey you take that money and get back to the kids. And hurry. I never did like that Gomez girl."

"She's okay."

"She smokes cigarettes. I saw her doing it once out back of the fire escape."

"Maria?" Helen's eyebrows shot up. "Smoking cigarettes?"

"Yep. Back of the fire escape."

"And you never told me?"

"Well I didn't—"

"I'll leave you two to settle this." Sweeney walked to a corner of his office, moved a table aside with his hip, kicked a rug out of the way, and lifted a plywood panel that covered a hole in the floor. Down inside the hole a safe sat, too heavy and awkward to move from that spot, which was why Sweeney put it there when he went into business in the first place. Sweeney dropped to his knees, dialed the combination quickly and opened the door. Looked down at the neat stacks of money within.

He quickly counted out forty twenties and went through the process of locking and hiding the safe again. Got his bulky body up with remarkable speed and even a touch of grace.

"Here you are, Helen," he said, handing her the stack of bills, beaming like a jovial department-store Santa trying to get a messy kid off his lap. "And be careful going home."

"This whole thing stinks on ice, ya crooked mick." She took the money, though, and turned back to Mort. "*You* be careful, hon. And come back to us quick."

There was something new in her eyes: growing respect, or maybe just the warm glow of holding all that money in her hands. Whatever it was, Mort drank it down like a hot, nourishing soup.

"See you soon, hon," he said. And, feeling a little embarrassed there in front of Brother Sweetie, he kissed his wife, picked up the keys and started through the door to the garage, weaving a little.

"Mort." Sweeney used his I'm-being-real-patient voice.

Mort stopped right where he was and turned to Sweeney.

"Leave the gun here, Mort."

Sheepishly, hoping he didn't look real dumb in front of Helen, Mort shuffled quickly to the desk and carefully, like a man does when he's not used to handling weapons, set down the snub-nose .38. Then he shuffled even more quickly back out to the garage.

"I hope he's up to it," Sweeney muttered.

"You listen to me." Helen started out the other door, to the parking lot, the street, her home and children. "That man can do anything he sets his mind to!" And then she was gone.

Less than a minute later, Sweeney lowered the garage door, watching Mort drive off in the ice truck. He was thoughtful as he returned to his office.

Let's see: got to pick out the right car for this next part. Something good in the snow, with a big trunk, that they can't trace back to me when they find it burned-out with the bodies inside. Maybe the '46 Chrysler. No, wait a minute; Boxer's got his own car and it's plenty big enough. Just use that....

He put on his overcoat, picked up the .38 from his desk and casually dropped it in his right-hand pocket. *Might as well do it quick and simple. Simple's always easy and quick is always quick. If this works out like I think it's going to...* He rifled quickly through the middle drawer and pulled out a blackjack, supple and worn from use. Stuck it up his right sleeve. *Hate to arrive at a party empty-handed.*

Let's see now. So I go out and I find Boxer first. Over to Lola's or close by there. Ask him if he's seen Mort, then kill him while he's trying to think up a lie. Nothing fancy. Get him in the trunk of his own car, then go out and collect Slimmy. He'll fit in the trunk too, fit just fine. But I better take the Chrysler just in case Boxer's won't start.

Outside of the garage, in the lot, he started up the '46 Chrysler that couldn't be traced back to him and sat inside thinking things over while it was warming up. *Find a good spot to leave Boxer's car once I get it all loaded up. Someplace where it won't get found quick but I can get back here easy, maybe the train station or— Hell, I got to be back here when Mort shows up with Walter and Eddie and all my money….*

He settled himself behind the wheel of the now-warm Chrysler, adjusted the mirror and headed downtown, reflecting that there was never enough time to get everything done around the holidays.

Chapter 45
Ten Hours and Thirty-Five Minutes
After the Robbery

December 20, 1951
7:35 PM
Eddie

It wasn't easy finding my way around a strange hospital, but I tried to look for the places with the most lights and the most folks running around wearing white. Anyone tried to stop me, I flashed my badge and looked busy. And I finally found what I was after.

Callie was in a room by herself, and someone had turned the lights low so she could rest better. A nurse was tapping a bottle that hung over her head with a tube dripping something into a vein in her arm. And there was a rubber breathing mask strapped over her face while a machine pumped air in. Kept her quiet, too, that mask did.

And that's what struck me all at once sad about it: the quiet in that room. And the stillness. No sound but the oxygen machine shoving air in her lungs and pulling it back out again. Nothing else moving at all but that nurse, gliding around like somebody's ghost.

I can't really say how I felt then. I mean, here was this woman I'd seen moving around like it hurt her to stand still, and talking like it pained her to shut up, and that was just a couple hours ago, and now here she was.

So damn still.

So damn quiet.

Something about it, it bothered me more than I figured. Funny, me taking on like that. I wiped my eyes and flashed my badge at the nurse. "How's Ranger Nixon doing?"

"Miss Callie?" she smiled at me. Nurses and cops just naturally get along, working nights and seeing blood like they do. "Doctor Woodrum said she's out of danger."

"Did they take the bullet out?"

"You must be really worried about her." She smiled again, the standard smile they keep tucked away and bring out for anxious relatives. "They're going to let her rest a little first. Doctor Woodrum will see to her in a couple of hours."

"Woodrum hurt himself," I said, "better call Doctor Robbins to do it."

"Doctor Robbins?" Her face showed what she thought of that idea, and it wasn't much.

"He's what you've got," I said. "Go get someone to page him." She still looked funny about it, so I added, "He'll surprise you."

For just a split second I thought she was going to put up a fight about it, but then she kind of shrugged her shoulders and walked out to do like I said.

That was what I wanted. I wanted to say something to Callie before I got the hell out of there. Couldn't figure what, though. And she likely wouldn't hear it anyway.

"Callie," I finally managed, "they say you're going to be fine. You're going to do just fine."

And then it was like something from an old monster movie when that big left hand of hers come up from under the sheet and pulled the oxygen mask right off her face.

"Can't you keep from lying to me?" she whispered.

"No lie," I said, "Doc Robbins, he just told me the bullet's where they can get it easy and, uh, they'll get it out of you easy he said, and…."

"And you're J. Edgar Hoover in disguise." Her voice was weak, not firm and classy like I was used to hearing it. And it was like she couldn't keep her eyes focused. She squinted at me.

"You're not in uniform, Officer Drapp."

"They promoted me to plain clothes," I said. "Now you just rest."

"I've got to—" She stopped to take a breath. "This is rather important, please. Can you listen?"

"All ears here."

"I know you robbed that bank or armored car or whatever it was, so you must be rather a desperate character and all." She stopped to breathe again. "But you brought me here so perhaps you could—" She stopped real sudden, like there wasn't any air, and she brought that black rubber mask back up to her face and took some air from it, took it in deep.

"You just rest," I said.

She pulled the oxygen mask back away from her face. "This is rather important," she said again, so I guessed it must be rather important—to her anyway. "I'm Catholic," she said, "I— that is, I quit believing in God back in college, all of us girls did, but aside from that I've always been a good Catholic, and I want a priest. I have a great deal to confess, I'm afraid."

"You don't need no priest," I said, "Doctor Robbins says—"

"Will you for the love of Fred please just do it?"

"I will." I put a hand on her shoulder to kind of quiet her. "But you got to rest."

And she did it. Like all of a sudden everything went out of her and her head laid back on that pillow like a balloon runs out of air.

"Promise me?" She whispered it, all faint and far away.

I put the oxygen mask back on her face and snugged it up good. Listened to her breathing, long and deep.

"Have I ever lied to you?"

But she didn't hear.

Chapter 46
Ten Hours and Forty-Eight Minutes
After the Robbery

December 20, 1951
7:48 PM
Boxer Healey

In his room above Lola's, Boxer Healey packed the last of his clean starched shirts carefully into the shiny-smooth natural rawhide Samsonite suitcase borrowed from Lola herself. Then he took his time rolling up neckties and tucking them neatly in the corners, telling himself he wasn't afraid of Brother Sweetie.

….the day I couldn't take that big pink blob is when I oughta just give up being a man and start crawling around him like everybody else in this no-account town….

He went to the closet one last time and picked out a good overcoat.

Still, there ain't no good reason to stick here and let him make things hard for me. Not with the weather so good down in Memphis this time of year and trains pulling out every hour.

He laid his coat across the bed and snapped the lock closed on the suitcase.

And as he did he heard another click, from the door.

Thought I locked that—know I did….

For half of a split second he considered spinning around and swinging his left at whoever must be in the room behind him. He knew this room and its dimensions as well as he ever knew any boxing ring, and his chances of getting in a fast, unexpected punch were pretty good.

Nah, he reasoned, *might just be Lola come to kiss me goodbye. I got time to turn around slow and act polite.*

He turned and saw he was wrong.

Bud Sweeney was in the room, moving fast up to where Boxer was still turning around, off balance. Before he could move again, he felt Sweeney's big left arm around his shoulders, pulling him close, and the snub-nose .38, the one Sweeney kept for social occasions, pressed against his chest, up high, just over his heart where a shot wouldn't cause too much bleeding. He just had time to appreciate that Brother Sweetie always did plan things out far ahead when he heard the last thing in his life as Sweeney smiled at him and said,

"Merry Christmas, Boxer."

Chapter 47
Ten Hours and Fifty Minutes
After the Robbery

December 20, 1951
7:50 PM
Eddie

I got back to the place in the hospital where I first came in, and there was Drapp and two deputies with two of those beds on wheels, and they was piled high with my ill-gotten gains.

"Before you go," he said, "have you seen anything of that auxiliary officer from Piketon? The one that drove all this in?"

I wondered why he wondered. Hoped he hadn't been figuring all this through.

"He's back in the operating room with that ranger-lady," I said. "She's talking now."

That turned his lights on.

"She is? What's she saying?"

"Keeps fading in and out," I said, "but from what I can gather, she got a lot of help from that guy...." Doc Robbins was just then rolling Walter out, right where I needed him, and beaming like a Boy Scout because he was all fixed up like I told him, with a coat on and his hands bandaged and his feet padded up in a big pair of rubber overshoes.

"Thank you so much, Doctor," I said. "We can take it from here."

"This is the guy that came in with the ranger-lady?" Drapp asked me.

Doc smiled, a little uncertain, "You're sure he, uh—"

And then a voice came over a loudspeaker in the ceiling, "Doctor Robbins, please report to the Operating Room," and repeated it to make sure there was no mistake. "Doctor Robbins, please report for surgery to the Operating Room."

From the look on his face I guessed he hadn't heard that in a while.

"Yeah," I said to Drapp. "Hang on a sec—" I turned back to Robbins. "Before you go," I said, "you got a priest or something hangs around here?"

"I, um, yes, Father Flaghtski is on call at all times…"

"Get him," I said, "that ranger-lady wants to see him before you take the bullet out. Just in case."

"I'm taking the bullet out?" He said it thoughtful, like he was trying to remember how far back it was the last time anyone asked him for anything important.

I stepped close and patted him on the shoulder, all friendly-like. Did he screw up operating on Callie I was going to come back, and him and me we'd have us a long talk about it, but no sense saying that now and getting him nervous, time like this. So I just said, "She wants that priest, Doctor. But you just make sure he won't have to do any last rites or anything like that. Make sure of it."

"I took bullets out in the war." I wasn't sure if he was talking to me or to himself, or to somebody no one could see, maybe. "I took so many bullets out of those men. Sometimes it seemed that was all I'd ever do again."

"Then you ought to get it done right, and no problem." Behind me, Drapp made an impatient noise.

"I shall need another drink." Robbins' eyes focused. "Just one. And just a small one." He looked at me and then at Drapp. "Goodbye for now, gentlemen."

He scooted off like a puppy that's done good, and I could get my mind back to Drapp.

"So I figure we book this one on suspicion," he said and looked down at Walter. "Just to keep him handy till we work this out. Can't go too far wrong arresting one of them."

"Sounds reasonable to me," I said. "We can always drop it later, or just vag him, do we need to. But we don't want that armored-car guard—" I was careful to say *we* so Drapp wouldn't think I was running this thing. Or trying to. "—that guy Pierce or whatever his name is—we don't want him getting too close to this one till we get this sorted out. I don't suppose you could keep him here any longer?"

Drapp grinned. "I told him we lost his statement," he said, "and said he had to write it out again. And I said we needed his prints to process the bags. Should be good for another two hours."

"Sharp work." I could have patted him on the head. "Have you arranged transport?"

"Wait till you see!"

So he walked me outside, along with four cops carrying the money bags, and it was a sure-enough pre-war paddy wagon, like you see in the old-time movies: a big metal prison on wheels with a peep-hole out the back and running boards with handles for cops to hang on to when they come charging down the street. Just looking at it sent me a deep-down shiver, and all the while the music outside was playing,

> *For hate is strong*
> *And mocks the song*
> *Of peace on Earth,*
> *Good will to men*

I helped Walter into the front seat while all the cops started throwing money bags into the back, then Drapp locked it up and handed me the key.

"You now have custody of the evidence," he said. "Andy here can drive you to the station."

Which is how come I to meet Andy.

He looked like the kind of guy that, was you doing something important, you'd want to put him someplace out of the way where he couldn't stick his foot in it. He gave me a big happy grin and pumped my hand and then he climbed behind the wheel and got a load of Walter.

"What's this?" he asked it so simple and innocent I wondered maybe he'd never seen a black man before. But I just told him it was an important witness and we had to take him to the station with us. And damn if he didn't slap Walter across the shoulder and give him that same grin as he gave me and he said, "Well, welcome along for the ride, Smokey!"

The cops all got inside out of the cold—Drapp, he practically ran in to get to talk with Callie, he thought—so there we was, just me and Walter...and Andy.

Well, it had been a good show, but I didn't figure to hang around and do any encores. I went over to the ranger truck, the one I drove us in on, and I fished around back behind the seat and came up with the shotgun. It was good and thawed out now, and I racked the chamber empty, snapped the trigger just to check it out, then loaded it up again, pushing shells into the magazine till it wouldn't hold no more.

And then the back door to the hospital flew open and somebody charged out yelling, "Hold it! You guys don't move!"

I leveled the shotgun.

It was the reporter. The one saw me when I first got here.

I moved closer to the ranger truck, where the shadows covered me a little, and hugged the shotgun close up to me, where I could step close and get off a shot quick, did I need to. And that reporter he just kept coming out the back of the hospital at us, and then I saw he was dragging something.

I stood a little easier. Not much, just a little.

"You guys forgot this bag—the one they left in the truck!"

And it was that last bag, the one that wouldn't fit in the car this morning, ten hours back and a lifetime ago.

I was glad to see it, but this was still a touchy situation. I grunted, "In here," and moved to the back of the paddy wagon where I quick opened the door and stood just a little in back of it.

Andy, god bless him, he jumped out of the driver's seat, grabbed that bag and threw it in the back. "Don't get too close," he said, real important, "all this is evidence, here."

"I don't care if it's Shinola," the reporter snapped back at him. "You guys would have left it here and had to make another trip if I hadn't stopped you."

I'd already closed the door back shut by then, and I stood behind Andy, keeping that big hat mostly over my face, I hoped. And holding the shotgun ready.

"Well, you never should have picked it up to start with," Andy was getting himself warmed up now. "A civilian's got no business getting his hands all over the evidence like that."

"Well, if some cops I know didn't leave it sitting around to walk off with, maybe we citizens wouldn't get our hands on it at all," the reporter said, but I nudged Andy, still standing close behind him, keeping out of sight, and I grunted again:

"Let's move out."

He looked at the reporter like he was going to really set him down a peg, could he think of something clever, but that was pretty far beyond him. I think he was glad of the excuse to leave. Then that reporter he looks close at me through the shadows.

"Who's this, anyway?"

"This is Mister None-Of-Your-Damn-Business, mister, that's who it is," Andy huffed. Which only got the reporter more interested in me.

"I'm Ned Nathan from the *Bootheville Daily*." The reporter stepped closer. "Can I get your name for the story, sir?"

Behind him, the music played,

Then pealed the bells more loud and deep,
God is not dead, nor doth he sleep,
The wrong shall fail, the right prevail…

And I don't think I ever saw a man walk so close to getting his face tore off with a shotgun as right then; I was just that near to doing it. But I leaned into him and half-whispered, "Meet me at the station. You won't believe this!"

His eyes didn't quite goggle at me—he'd been too long a reporter for that, I guess. But his jaw almost dropped and he started, "Hey, aren't you the guy—?"

I shushed him, trying to look subtle about it. The same like I had with Drapp, like I was letting him in on a secret. I flashed him the badge and held it out there long enough for him to get a good look—because I knew he couldn't see it in the dark.

"Wait till you hear it," I half-whispered. "At the station."

And it worked. He was on to a sharp angle on this big story, he figured, and that was enough to shut him up and keep him happy.

Next thing, we were all three of us in the front seat: me, Walter and Andy, and Andy was backing us out of that parking lot, driving slow because the streets still looked like trouble. While he did it, I jacked a round into the chamber of that shotgun and flipped the safety.

"Da-yam," Andy said, and he grinned at me but kept his eyes on the road, "you must be expecting trouble!"

"Well you never can tell." I smiled back at him. "Can you?"

"Guess not." He let the clutch out, felt the wheels slide then bite into the slush as we headed out onto the snowplowed street. "So, whatcha doing for Christmas?"

Chapter 48
Thirty Years After the Robbery

July 14, 1981
Eddie

But all that's starting to be a long time ago.

Walter and me, we got the money to Brother Sweetie, and he paid us off on the spot. Always a sunuvabitch but a good man to do business with, that was Brother Sweetie. I worked with guys in my time—back when I was doing work like that, I mean—worked with guys you oughta split the loot up first thing, 'cause if you waited till later you had to go to all the trouble of splitting them off your share. Not Brother Sweetie; he was always honest in his ways, or he was till some dope fiend blew his stomach out about ten years back, which is getting off the subject.

So like I said, we got óur money, and I done the next couple weeks taking care of Walter till his hands and feet got better. Of course we were nowhere close to Willisburg or Bootheville by then; we was short in those towns, and we'd moved a couple good states away, but I kept checking the out-of-town newspaper stand, and funny thing was, there was plenty of news in the papers from Willisburg and Bootheville about the big armored-car robbery, but nothing about what went on that night in the hospital. Not one word. So I guess somebody owed that reporter a favor. Or maybe he owed them. Anyway, they hushed it all up about how I got away with the money, and that suited me just fine. Just after Christmas there was something about how the cops had put out warrants for arrest in the case, but when I read the story it was about how nobody had seen Slimmy Johnson and Boxer Healey, two local characters, it said, ever since the day of the robbery. I guess the cops figured them leaving town right after the armored car shed all that weight, well, they figured the two things might tie in together. But a couple months later when the weather got warm, there was another story about how those two had spent the winter in the trunk of Boxer's car, sitting in a crowded parking lot. They might not have found them even then, but some guy who made his living breaking into cars turned them up and then went and told the cops about it. The papers said they let him go—the guy who found them I mean, they let him go—which was probably a bad thing, to let someone that dumb out walking the streets, but that's none of my business.

Anyway we got along pretty good, Walter and me, while he was healing up, I mean, and I talked him around to coming up to Akron with me when I bought into that gas station. From what he said, I figured Walter to be a good man with a hook, so we went in on buying a tow-truck together and with him towing wrecks and break-downs for me to fix up, it brought in more business. Come to it, work got pretty steady there. I even put up a sign that said,

> WE OFFER WORK THAT IS
> CHEAP
> FAST
> RELIABLE
> YOU CAN HAVE ANY TWO

And we did pretty good. An honest mechanic gets good word of mouth pretty quick, and I was fairly honest, for a mechanic. Not like in the old days. That was all behind me then. It had to be.

After a while, Walter and me went down south a ways to someplace about fifty miles uphill from Absolutely Nowhere and Walter picked up his brother's wife—Gypsy, her name was—and her kids, and moved them up to Akron with us. I think he married her, but I never knew for sure. He raised those kids like they was his own, though, that much I know. They always called him Popaw.

Me, I got married a couple times, but it never took. Funny, both of them told me the same thing when they left: said it was like I was keeping something back from them, something important-like and they never could get me to share it.

Well yeah, I guess so.

I mean, do you marry a decent woman, you don't just go telling her how you got your start in business by robbing and killing, and shot some guy's ear off once. And I sure wouldn't marry some tramp. Walter's woman put it good: Him and me was sipping a beer in his kitchen right after the second one left me, and Gypsy up and says, "Trouble with you, you don't want any woman that would have a man like you for a husband, that's all."

And I guess she got it right.

But there was something else besides, which was that I never got Callie off my mind: that big ugly ranger-lady back in the park there. Maybe it was how she saved my life that kept me thinking at her—it sure wasn't sex appeal. You know how you look back on something bad and years later on it don't seem as awful as it did right at the time. Like I still remembered the sight of all those Germans, back at Bastogne, running up the hill at us, but it didn't seem as scary anymore as it did back then. But when I thought back on Callie she still looked ugly enough to stampede buffalo. So I can't figure why sometimes I'd just get to wondering whatever become of her, and I couldn't put it out my mind.

I mean, she didn't die or nothing. That was the first thing I looked for in the papers, and when I read they had her listed in satisfactory condition, I felt pretty good about it. And I felt better when I read some further about how she said she couldn't remember nothing about what happened that day on account of she'd lost so much blood.

That left the cops trying to figure out what Captain Scranton had to do with everything; trying to see how him getting burned all to hell tied in with the truck I stole off that farmer and left there in the park. And how all that ended up with some part-time cop nobody knew nothing about—how he dropped off the money and a black man, and then everything disappeared and Healey and Johnson climbed into the trunk of a car for the winter....

Well it was kind of a mess, what with them getting that description from the armored-car guards, looking for two guys in an ambulance, and I'm not surprised they never did hit the bottom of it.

I always kind of wondered though, did Callie really not remember what happened or was she maybe covering for me?

Never did find out.

So like I say it kind of stuck in my mind some, and then last year Walter fell over dead. Damnedest thing. He'd just come up towing somebody's Mustang and he bent over the switch to lower the hook and just kept bending over till I found him like that and the doctor said it was a massive coronary and he likely never knew he was dying till he looked down from Heaven and saw he was dead. Damnedest thing. And boy did they carry on at his funeral.

Well, that got me thinking at my own health, and why I was coughing all the time lately. So I looked up a good doctor, and he sent me to another doctor, and that one sent me for some X-rays and when I come back he told me I had a cancer growing in my chest. No surprise, considering I'd smoked a pack of Luckies every day since I was twelve. Didn't figure to stop, either. I just thanked the doctor for his time and checked out.

And the next thing I was on a plane to Willisburg Airport and then rented a car and drove out to Boothe National Park.

It was on one of those days that's just fine for going to the park; not too hot but plenty of sun. The ranger station was a brand new thing, which shouldn't have surprised me since the old knotty-pine office would have been food for the termites by now, but I got kind of a funny feeling when I walked in the big, square-shiny Formica-and-plastic ranger office and asked did anyone remember Calpurnia Nixon.

Well, the ranger I asked, he was a young guy—they pretty much all are, anymore. He had an Army crew-cut and a know-everything look on him, and he just smiled a crooked kind of smile and said, "You're a month too late, man."

I looked at him, and something in my face sobered him up and he looked behind him and said, "Jennie, this guy wants to know about Captain Callie."

Up pops a smart-looking young lady and she's dressed in a uniform that hasn't changed much since the last time I saw one.

"Did you know Captain Nixon?" she asked.

It wasn't funny anymore to find a woman in a job like this, but just seeing her there in that uniform like that, well it really took me back.

"Met her once," I said. "She guided me through the park here and…and I guess that's all there is to it. Just wondered was she still around, but the way you put it I guess she ain't."

"Her ashes are," she said. "We scattered them in the woods here last month."

Oh.

Well, that shut me up while the ranger told me how Callie worked there these last thirty years, and it was always kind of her park, and she looked to see it was the best park she could make it. Like the trees and animals there was something special to her. Then one day she just told Jennie here she was going away and Jennie should mind things, and then she went up a trail into the woods.

"We found her the next morning," Jennie told me, "lying under a tree. She had such a peaceful look on her face, and the animals hadn't touched her at all. It was like she sat down there to rest and just went away. Like she said."

"An easy death," I said.

"Funny you should say that." The young girl gave me the look she likely got out and showed to all the old fossils. "It was an expression she used a lot: an easy death."

"Yeah, I guess it's funny," I said. "Is there a marker anyplace?"

"She wouldn't have one," the girl said. "That was very clear in her will. She just wanted her ashes scattered around the park where she'd spent her life, so that's what we did."

"You know," I said, looking through one of the big windows out at the woods beyond, "back when she first started to work here, it wasn't easy for a woman to get a job like this."

"I've read about things like that." She smiled. "I took a course on Women's Issues in college."

Well, that made me feel like I'd just stepped out of a Civil War photograph.

"So there's no marker?" I asked again, just to make myself feel a little less dead.

The guy behind her spoke up. "The only marker in the park is a big old granite thing up by where the lookout tower used to be," he said. "And it's for some guy no one remembers."

✿

It was well into afternoon by the time I got out to that marker where the ranger tower had been, so long ago. There was nothing there now but a big, stone-block thing, the kind of monument they used to think was impressive back in the 1950s, and on it they'd put up a brass plaque:

> ### TO THE MEMORY
> ### OF
> ### CAPTAIN ALVIN P. SCRANTON
> ### JUNE 3, 1921 – DEC. 20, 1951
> ### WHO GAVE HIS LIFE IN THIS PARK

I tried to figure on it some: This guy Scranton, I guess I never got to know him good except he was a crazy-mean sunuvabitch who'd kick a man when he was down, and never took his job serious except that it give him his chance to shoot animals easier—and he didn't mind the notion of setting me on fire, either. And here they'd put up this big monument to his life or something.

Callie, she was the kind of woman that stayed in your mind, ugly as she was, and that was in a good way, and I figured she'd worked pretty hard at doing whatever you do to a place like this, but there wasn't any marker over her at all. Nothing to show she'd ever been there except maybe the park itself and the great-great grand-puppies of some dumb animals she'd kept from getting killed.

Time to come, everybody'd likely forget about her, but they'd always see this big stone marker for the guy I killed.

That means something, but I just don't figure it.

Don't Let the Mystery End Here.
Try These Other Great Books From
HARD CASE CRIME!

Hard Case Crime brings you gripping, award-winning crime fiction
by best-selling authors and the hottest new writers in the field.
Find out what you've been missing:

FIFTY-to-ONE
by CHARLES ARDAI

Written to celebrate the publication of Hard Case Crime's 50th book, *Fifty-to-One* imagines what it would have been like if Hard Case Crime had been founded 50 years ago, by a rascal out to make a quick buck off the popularity of pulp fiction.

A fellow like that might make a few enemies—especially after publishing a supposed non-fiction account of of a heist at a Mob-run nightclub, actually penned by an 18-year-old showgirl with dreams of writing for *The New Yorker*.

With both the cops and the crooks after them, our heroes are about to learn that reading and writing pulp novels is a lot more fun than living them...

ACCLAIM FOR CHARLES ARDAI

"A very smart and very cool fellow."
— Stephen King

"Charles Ardai...will be the next me but, I hope, less peculiar."
— Isaac Asimov

Available now at your favorite bookstore.
For more information, visit
www.HardCaseCrime.com

Classic Suspense from

Donald E. Westlake's Legendary Alter Ego

Lemons
NEVER LIE

by RICHARD STARK

When he's not pulling heists with his friend Parker, Alan Grofield runs a small theater in Indiana. But putting on shows is expensive and jobs have been thin, which is why Grofield agrees to listen to Andrew Myers' plan to knock over a brewery in upstate New York.

Unfortunately, Myers' plan is insane—so Grofield walks out on him. *But Myers isn't a man you walk out on…*

RAVES FOR 'LEMONS NEVER LIE'

"This first-rate hard-boiled mystery…reads like Raymond Chandler with a dark literary whisper…of Cormac McCarthy."
— Time

"The prose is clean, the dialogue laced with dry humor, the action comes hard and fast."
— George Pelecanos

"Lemons Never Lie is a delight— a crime story that leaves you smiling."
— Washington Post

"The best Richard Stark ever."
— Paul Kavanagh

Available now at your favorite bookstore.
For more information, visit
www.HardCaseCrime.com